US
FOR THE

Us for the Night

C R Y S T A L
◆ PUBLISHING ◆

Dedication:

A very special thank you to the writers group "Stupid AM Writing", who wake up before the sun rises every morning. Thank you for your support and cheerleading as we follow our dreams and write down words before the day starts. And a huge thank you to my readers who keep the dream alive. Thank you x

Chapter 1

Sotiny

My temperament was already taut. A lot was riding on this meeting with Hayden Zilch, and to top it off I had to deal with Alex as well? Someone give me strength, because I was going to need it.

I smiled politely at the new barista who repeated back my order as I handed her my money. It was my usual order, the same time every morning, right before I went into the office.

As if someone had a vendetta against me personally, the devil himself walked in, the small bell above the door ringing as Alex strode in as if he owned the place. I began biting my thumbnail trying to calm my already irritated nerves. I purposefully stepped out of the way, hoping by chance he didn't see me as I fabricated sudden interest in their limited-edition mugs.

"You're new here," Alex purred to the young, perky brunette behind the counter. My jaw clenched of its own accord. His velvety smooth-as-chocolate voice would have most women on their knees. As I briefly glanced back, it was doing exactly that to the newcomer. Another victim of Alex Fields.

Alex flashed her that devilish smile—the one that promised guilty pleasures and something you just wouldn't quite come back from. Such a shame he'd sleep with her only once and throw her to the side. That was his rule, after all.

I adjusted my thick winter coat and tried to bury the lower half of my face. The coffee mug almost slipped through my hands as his piercing green eyes fixed on mine as I peeked again. My heartbeat sped up, as it always did when I first took him in and then it was overtaken by an unrequited and underestimated rage.

"You really should stop biting your nails," Alex critiqued as he walked over to stand by my side. Without realizing, I pulled my thumb away from my mouth. The new barista watched on in interest.

With jaw clenched, I gritted out, "I don't think *you* should be a person to offer such criticism."

"Oh? Pray tell, how could anyone criticize me?" He asked, running his hand casually down himself cockily. This man was intolerable. And was indefinitely wearing the same cologne I'd once confessed scattered my thoughts. Everything about him was insufferable.

"Perhaps should we start with your crude behaviour of eye fucking every barista that starts at our local coffee spot," I seethed so quietly, only he could hear.

"Eye fucking?" His eyebrows perked up in shock. "Miss Granger, I never knew you had that vocabulary in your repertoire."

"Don't call me that," I sniped, my tone filled with acid. He knew I hated that nickname he'd given me ever since I was a teen. Okay, yes, I loved Harry Potter but that wasn't the reason why he started the nickname. He'd always called me a "Goody Two-Shoes" and when he realized the joke irked me, he'd continued it ever since.

"You found it cute once," he said somberly. "And I wasn't eye fucking anyone."

"Sotiny," the barista called out. With a polite smile, I grabbed my coffee and briefed a glance down at his. In small writing, a number was written on top of his coffee. *Seriously? That easily?*

"Alex," she sang out with a smooth voice.

"Have a good day, Sotiny," the owner called out as I made my leave. With a polite smile and curt nod, I walked out. The heels however prevented me from creating any real distance between us. Within a few seconds, Alex was beside me.

I tucked myself further into my jacket, avoiding the cold bite of winter. More to the point, I was trying to hide away from Alex.

"Why are you following me?" I grumbled.

"Come on, Sots. Surely you can retract the claws on a Friday? Who can possibly wake up on a Friday so... uptight?"

"Any day I wake knowing that I have to deal with you is what makes me so 'uptight,'" I grumbled. Everything about him wound me up into a taut irritation.

He daringly stepped in front of me. "C'mon, just for today can we put the knives away?"

The hustling city of Manhattan continued around us in a swirl of noise and sunrise between tall buildings. And although I was certain time contin-ued, it felt like it was just us. Especially when he stood so close. And that was the problem. I hated myself more for the reaction my body had to him.

Alex was hardly ever early and by way of the

gym bag hanging on his side, I knew he'd already been working out at his local boxing gym. Alex Fields was never early to work. The only reason he'd step foot in here so early was if he deemed something important or to gain from. Like today's meeting. But that was yet again the problem, he was good at everything—including his job and this project we'd been forced to work on together. My grip tightened.

He continued, as if my way of silence was promising. "We meet with Hayden Zilch today, shouldn't we go over some notes?"

Every time he spoke, my hackles raised. He was so used to women fawning over him and agreeing to his whims. I refused.

I stepped around him. "There's no need, we've emailed enough suggestions and articulated how this meeting will go. The execution will be just as exact."

Alex growled, pushing his calloused hand through his dark-blonde hair. "You're so uptight. Just work with me for once."

The click of my heels was the audible sound of my defiance—every step.

"You do realize we have to talk about this like adults at some point," he continued, despite the few onlookers on the street, curious about what probably seemed like a lovers' quarrel. I had the urge to smooth over my hair, ignoring him as he called out behind me.

I greeted the security guard and beelined for the elevator, pushing on the button feverishly.

"You can't always run away, Sotiny, we do work together now."

My neck whiplashed as I spun on him. I wanted to scream. He always knew what to say to goad me. He was the only person who could climb under my perfectly manicured frame and make me act irrationally.

I clipped my tone, restraining myself from exploding. "You think I'm running away?" I hissed, my entire jumble of thoughts no longer coherent. "Rich coming from you, wouldn't you say? What you didn't get enough from me? You want to patronize me more? See when I'll next combust?"

Alex seemed taken aback. "Sotiny, that's not what I meant."

"It might not be what you meant but it's what you do, Alex. You just push people's buttons unable to take no for an answer. This is the reaction you wanted, wasn't it?" A hot flush ran over me, as I pressed the elevator button three more times. *What was taking it so long?*

"I just... I want us to work together on this

project. I don't want our relationship to affect this project."

I scoffed. "If you think my dislike for you is interfering with my efficiency in my job, you're sadly mistaken. I just don't share the same desire to spoon-feed you the finer details. And FYI, you and I *don't* have any sort of relationship." With a frustrated growl, I pressed the call button twice more. "I'll take the stairs."

"No need." Alex pushed past me. "I'll take the stairs. I wouldn't want to add any more inconvenience onto your plate," he spited.

I held my resolve, defiantly watching him as he walked away. Somehow it felt better when he bit back. When he reminded me of the asshole he could be. When he was nice... when he was charming... when he was Alex Fields... that's what drove me nuts. And I had the audacious fate to not only have to work with him in the same office but on the same project every damn day.

Chapter 2

Alex

I stared down at the number written on my coffee cup and spaced out thinking of Sotiny's blue, scornful gaze and pursed lips. She was driving me into maddening oblivion. No matter how much I tried to shake her, that pole wasn't sliding out of her ass any time soon. She was just so tightly wound up, like a perfect little doll. A doll that I'd seen break once before.

"It's unlike you being here so early, what's the special occasion?" Clover remarked as she leant against my office doorframe. *Ever early and the teachers pet,* I thought. Well, as expected from our new travel columnist—not forgetting to mention, the CEO of *Be True* magazine's girlfriend. She might've been a new addition to our corporate family but she was a powerhouse, and I was happy for my best friend, Damon, to find himself such a woman. It was if nothing else hilarious to watch the hard exterior of Damon melt like butter whenever she was around.

"Well, you know early start and all I'm hoping the boss will let me off early. No bodyguard today?" I asked with a cocky smile, teeth flashing.

"Damon's already in his office." Clover smiled, all whites flashing, leveling my charm. She'd gotten used to me now, and I purposefully pushed Damon's buttons just to see what reaction I'd get from him.

"Hmmm maybe I can try to drag him out tonight in celebration of our big win today," I teased. It was a premature claim of course. Hayden Zilch hadn't yet signed any contract, but I was certain we'd secure him to be the face of our new sports magazine. We wanted someone with a public profile and the man had established himself as a sports manager and smart investor, building a billionaire empire. Hayden Zilch was all the craze and had great connections in the industry, and we couldn't have thought of anyone edgier to pave the way.

"Good luck dragging Damon out," Clover laughed. "But it might be good for him to get out of the house once in a while."

"I don't think he'll be leaving any house that

you're in anytime soon," I joked. She offered me a hesitant but coy smile. The two were absolutely head over heels for each other.

"You make me sound like a ball and chain," she joked before peering over her shoulder. Towering over her was the brooding Damon, as if summoned by sheer instincts that another man was talking to his woman. This slightly jealous side of him was rather refreshing to watch, and I couldn't help but poke at him like the big bear he was.

"What are you two talking about?" Damon asked as he pressed a kiss to Clover's cheek in greeting. She gave him a knowing smile and handed him his coffee.

"Clover was suggesting that we all go out tonight to celebrate," I replied, throwing my legs onto the desk casually and leaning back. I purposefully placed my hands on the back of my head, splaying my huge arms.

"Was she now?" Damon asked arching an eyebrow. He didn't doubt in our ability to acquire this contract and negotiations either. Despite Sotiny's and my differences, Damon and his sister and co-CEO, Michelle, had put us on this project together for a reason.

Clover bit her bottom lip, evidently trying not to laugh. "Something like that."

Damon ever so quietly whispered into her ear as he grabbed her hip. "But I thought we were going to watch that special movie tonight?"

"Yuck!" I kicked my feet off my table. "Hard no from me, you two take your office romance shenanigans somewhere else."

Clover chuckled as she grabbed Damon's hand. "Come on, you, we *actually* come to this office to *work*."

"Yea but you leave for your next trip in a week again," I heard Damon grumble as they walked down the hall. The guy had fallen hard.

Once I was alone, my smile faltered. I'd been best friends with Damon for over ten years now. I'd worked for *Be True* magazine as their advertising executive for all that time, been there for Damon's highs and lows, and where he'd changed... I'd unapologetically stayed the same. It was only eight in the morning but I felt that promise of a regular Friday night—drink, prowl and immersing in the high of Manhattan—hitting me already.

I grabbed the small basketball in my room and threw it into the hoop that was screwed into the wall. Without fail, it sank straight through. But first I simply needed to lock in this contract with Hayden Zilch.

Chapter 3

Sotiny

It was a "big dick energy" standoff to say the least. Were all men like this or only the extremely good-looking ones that had some alpha quota to prove? Hayden Zilch was fine, almost cut from the same cloth as Alex. Six foot two and built like a brickhouse of a jock still in his prime. The photos in magazines and articles did nothing to express the pure magnetism the man held. Light-sandy-blonde hair, a clean-shaven face, and piercing brown eyes that would lure any woman under a spell and that smile. That cocky, arrogant, playboy smile was all the same.

Many bystanders ogled as Hayden Zilch walked through the office while we stood here waiting to greet him. I wanted to eye roll Alex and Hayden, and tell them to either fight or fuck with the amount of tension the two held. This was not going to help our contract whatsoever.

"It's lovely to finally meet you," I said politely, offering my hand with a sharp smile. He took it; the warmth in his gaze pooling into me. I imagined most women fell for it, but I was already familiar with the charm of a playboy. Once you grew up with one, you built an intolerance to them all. "Sotiny Bryer. I hope the flight treated you well."

"It's lovely to finally meet the face that matches the voice over the phone," Hayden charmed. I could feel tension roll off Alex behind me; his obvious stare at our entwined hands—which he probably deems longer the necessary. It fuelled my irritation toward him, like he had any say in whom I chose to shake hands and spend my time with anyway.

"Likewise," I politely said, pulling back my hand and onto the stack of books and notes in my other arm, we'd been going over in our meeting. He wore a simple black suit and white shirt beneath. Despite his mid-thirties appearance, slightly accented charm, and billionaire profile, he seemed... normal. Not flashy or snobbish like some of the clients I'd onboarded, but just like a normal guy.

Hayden's gaze widened as he peered over my

shoulder. "Clover?" he gasped. His lips curled into a boyish smile. Alex and I shared a brief glance. Clover had mentioned they'd been college friends in Ithaca, but I could sense the palpable tension run through Damon, who was shadowing her. Despite his calm, stoic demeanor, when it came to Clover, he was as readable as a boy in love for the first time—especially while he hovered behind her. I tried not to smirk, thinking about how Alex often goaded him as her "bodyguard."

"Hayden?" Clover's face lit up in a youthful smile and she leapt for him, embracing the giant man as best she could. All formality and professionalism was gone but it could work to our advantage. "I haven't seen you since we graduated. Oh, my good-ness. Look at you," she remarked, pulling away and looking over him again.

"Now, that's not how you greet me. C'mon," he joked, holding his knuckles out. Their apparent secret handshake looked awkward at first, until muscle memory kicked in. I glanced Damon's way again, oddly finding humor in his stiff demeanor.

"Come on, as if that was ever it. Put more gusto in it." Hayden grabbed her hand and clenched it into a fist running over numerous gestures. He then raised his hand, expecting her to jump for it. "C'mon... you always jumped for it."

She laughed and pushed him away. "I'm not going to jump for it in heels and a pencil skirt. And besides I'm not that girl anymore, I don't know if my knees will keep up," she joked.

"Please, you look exactly the same as you did all those years ago, if not even better. And in those heels, if anything you could probably jump higher now," he challenged.

A low cough crept from Alex, presumably out of consideration for Damon who stood there frozen over. As if remembering they weren't alone, Clover quickly apologized.

"Sorry it's been so long," she mused. "This is Damon Brogardt our CEO."

Damon stepped forward and shook his hand. "Apologies, my sister and co-CEO, Michelle, couldn't join us today. She's recently had some health concerns. This must be rather refreshing for you two to meet again?"

Alex and I shared another glance. *He was definitely jealous.*

Clover charmed a smile. "It's been so long. Hayden and I used to study at Ithaca College together.

He and I attended some of the same lectures and had the same group of friends for a while." She seemed to drift off into nostalgic memories. "How is Veronica?"

Hayden looked to the ceiling for a moment, obviously trying to recall something before laughing. "Oh, Veronica. Pfft, that didn't last long. We broke up about a month after graduation. I think she's married with kids now."

"Wow, I'll have to social media stalk her," Clover said, wide-eyed. "She was always so prim and proper, the thought of her having children running around seems profound. I'm super excited to hear you might be joining us for the sports editions?"

Hayden's gaze flicked between Clover and Damon, as if picking up on the tension between the two. Although they never publicly displayed affection in front of others at the office, Hayden seemed to have a keen eye.

"Depending on how this meeting goes," he offered a polite smile.

"You won't regret it," Clover charmed. "Well, I think I've taken enough of your time. I'm about to grab another coffee. Would anyone else like one while I'm there?"

I shook my head. Only one a day for me or I'd be awake for the rest of the night.

"Still just a regular old Americano cup of joe?" Clover asked Hayden.

"Yea. Good to see you remembered."

Damon's gaze followed Clover for a moment longer, the lingering not missed by Hayden. I wanted to again roll my eyes, standing between the testosterone-filled standoff with three brutes for men.

"Shall we?" Alex charmed, then gestured toward the conference room.

Hayden clasped his hands together. "Let's do it."

Damon followed, his gaze shooting arrows at Alex who evidently was trying his hardest not to laugh at him. Where Damon held professionalism, Alex often let it slip when others weren't watching. He'd always been that meddlesome teenager, and I was certain some parts of him would never quite mature. Although I'd found it charming once I'd grown to realize it was one of his greatest downfalls.

He gestured for me to step forward first, his hand daringly pressing on the small of my back as he whispered into my ear, "This should be interesting." His hot breath flushed down my neck, spreading goose bumps over my body.

With gritted teeth and nose held high, I side-eyed him. Where my look had men at times groveling in apology, his smile only widened. "Indeed," I clipped. That one word enough to express, *if you don't remove that hand from my back, I'll sever it myself.*

He chuckled, as if reading my mind.

This meeting was designed to finalize all the negotiations and put the contracts in place. I'd been dealing with his assistant Amber for the past few months, based in his office in Ithaca. And without Michelle here, I took my representation as her personal assistant very seriously.

I sat across from Hayden, Damon opting to sit at the head of the table. And Alex annoyingly taking his place beside me. It was only in recent months that he'd become so brazen. We'd usually avoid standing in the same room together, let alone sitting side by side.

"It's a nice office here. I considered changing my main office to New York but enjoy Ithaca's charm," Hayden smoothed over.

"It could be the best of both worlds," Damon encouraged as he leant back in his chair, that same intimidating and yet somehow warm expression replicating his sister's. The Brogardt family had an air about them. I felt almost discouraged by how perfected they were in their meetings. I often found myself wondering if others could see through my cracks and the ugliness that lay within in comparison.

"That it could," Hayden considered. "I've gone over the contract; it doesn't look like it'll impact my schedule too much although my team will be heavily involved. I don't mind being the face of the project and I already have a few ideas that might work well in conjunction, as I've already suggested previously. I can't offer exclusive interviews with my players, but I can offer it to be the first on the press. As you know I have an extensive list of players in their prime across numerous fields, so it'll work in seasons as well."

"Understandably," Damon agreed.

"We're also happy to discuss any marketing or sponsorships you want to partner up with in the magazine," Alex stated. Already, the negotiations were floating about, most of what I'd already written in the draft contract was being agreed upon.

"And your agreement on the photo shoot for the first release?" I queried. We were moving this all pretty quickly. We were anticipating the first edition to release in only a matter of months, depending on Hayden Zilch's agreement.

"You had me the moment you said there would

be a grand party." Hayden cocked a smile. I smiled politely in return. I could feel Alex's gaze on me.

Casually, Hayden added, "I actually heard there's a few places that have opened up since I was last here?"

Alex chuckled. "Somethings always opening every weekend." He lazily leant forward collecting his pen and noting down something. I incredulously tried to make out the small font with little success.

"Perhaps Alex could take you tonight, he's always out on a Friday night," I said with a sharp smile. Alex's gaze fell on me. It was general knowledge Alex spent his weekends out socializing. "Socializing" being code for hooking up. From one girl to another, he could have anyone he wanted. Weren't these two men a match for one another? And any kind of friendly relationship was a bonus for us.

"That's correct. I suppose I could take you. I was actually discussing with Clover this morning that we should all go out tonight so that works just fine."

Damon's expression went stone-cold and I tried my hardest not to snort at his icy demeanor.

"Really?" Hayden said, interested. "I think I'd really enjoy that. I'm here for the weekend so why not."

"Indeed," I agreed.

With an impression of a smile, Damon said, "And Sotiny was just saying it's been a while since she'd been out and about, so I think it'd be a perfect excursion for you to come out as well." Alex seemed to pale.

My pen stilled in my hand, my notes coming to a stop. With a clenched jaw, I tried forcing another polite smile. I couldn't outright deny my boss. But I was so obviously being dragged in as collateral damage because of Alex's little games.

"Perfect," I lied.

My gaze landed on Alex's with the wrath of everything I promised to come. He took a heavy gulp.

Satisfied, Damon continued, suddenly merrier than when he'd come into this room, "Okay, let's continue going over the finer details."

The finer details were in way of how I was going to chop Alex into tiny pieces and feed him to the fishes.

Chapter 4

Alex

He got me. Despite how begrudging Damon had been about me ruining his "special movie night," he seemed to be beaming at the prospect of Sotiny now coming out as well. I was certain he'd find humor in my uncomfortableness as much as I did watching him get jealous over Hayden and Clover reliving past times.

I was first to arrive, downing a stiff drink to take the edge of. Manhattan on a Friday night was the highlight of my week. But this changed everything. Despite it being winter, women still wore elegantly decorated short dresses on the rooftop bar. Snow globe-like domes, like private rooms, decorated the rooftop bar—in summer, it was cabanas instead.

I opted to hire out a private booth in their garden bar adorned with wild foliage and chandeliers. It was only a few minutes past nine, and yet the place was almost at full capacity. Waitresses in tropical attires sauntered around bottles at a time. I shrugged my leather jacket off, overheating by the discreet heaters already. I threw back the rest of my whisky. I was going to need another double pronto if I was ever going to survive this night.

When everyone arrived, I planned to be in and out, straight down to the club two levels down.

"Another one, sir?" the polite waitress asked with a seductive smile. Had it been any other night, I might've reciprocated the attention, but I was not up for my actions being ridiculed tonight by a certain little uptight miss.

"Yes please." With a disappointed smile she took my glass. "Actually, please make it two."

Fuck how *was* I going to survive this night?

My cell buzzed and I looked down at the simple text from Damon. *Running late.* A grunt rippled through me. He better not have bailed. No doubt the two were late because they couldn't keep their hands off one another.

"Alex?" A high tone grabbed my attention and a

cold chill swept over me. *Fuck.* Why were the Olsen twins here tonight of all nights? "We never heard back from you after that night?"

Without an invite, they slipped into either side of my booth. Beneath the identical charming smiles, the two were vipers in a den. They were notorious for grabbing men with money, chewing them up and spitting them out to bleed.

"Maybe you were both too much for me to handle," I joked, eyeing the direction the waitress had gone in, praying she'd arrive with my drink sooner.

"It certainly didn't seem like that," one of them pouted. The truth was, I couldn't tell them apart. Ashley and Courtney were their names. And I never asked questions beyond that.

"We'd like it if maybe you could handle us again," the other agreed. Her hand slipped over my inner thigh, her long, manicured nails digging in. My cock throbbed at the thought, the memories vivid. Yes, it was a night I'd remembered. But that was my rule, only once, no strings attached.

And this would only complicate things if Sotiny walked in, especially when—

A long cream coat caught my attention and those piercing blue eyes narrowed on my compromising position. *Fuck.* How was it I had the worst timing?

Behind her, like a giant, Hayden loomed. Sotiny stopped at the table, her gaze lasered into me and then the two women.

I was so fucked.

A small smirk twisted Hayden's lips as he looked away as if preoccupied. *What was he smirking at?* A cold chill rippled through me at Sotiny's potent gaze.

"He's alright too," one of the twins whispered to other, leaning over me as she pointed to Hayden.

"Remove yourself from this booth," Sotiny pointedly said, that acid-like tone of hers chilling.

"Excuse me? And you are?" the twin whose hand was grasped near my cock asked. The word "fuck" found itself on a repetitive loop in my mind.

"I don't have time for this," Sotiny said to me specifically, all hatred and rage in that gaze of hers. "We're here for a work function with our new client and you're in the way." As if remembering she was in public, she offered a smile that was not at all polite. It was all fangs and cruel intent. The girls blanched. Of course only us three were victim to it. She had her back to Hayden, ensuring that no one else would see this "unrefined" version that she tried to keep hidden so deeply.

"Whatever, call us later, okay?" One of the twins winked at me.

"And I wouldn't mind if you joined us," the other flirted, placing her hand on Hayden's chest. He offered a polite enough smile.

"Nice friends you have there," Hayden commented.

"There not my friends," I quickly blurted.

"It sure looked friendly to me," Sotiny clipped as the waitress walked over. Before she could even place the two glasses on the table Sotiny collected them. "Thank you. Do you drink whisky, Hayden?"

He seemed bemused by our tension as he darted a glance between the two of us. "I do."

She handed him one.

"You don't even like whisky," I grumbled, the cold sweat finally breaking.

"I do now," she replied. Her makeup was slightly heavier than usual, but not enough to conceal the few freckles that scattered her nose. Her strawberry-blonde hair was perfectly straightened as usual.

The waitress seemed confused and reluctantly, I gestured my fingers for another two whiskeys. "And a pina colada as well please. That's still your favourite isn't it?"

Silence. Cold shoulder. Tonight was off to a great start already.

"Did you two used to date?" Hayden asked.

"No," we both said in unison.

Another smirk crossed his face. The waitress sauntered off, and I begrudgingly stared at Sotiny as she took a mouthful of my whisky and downed it. By way of her wince, I knew she still hated the stuff.

Hayden seemed impressed, following suit. "Well, if it's going to be one of those nights, why not?" He threw it back. "I'll go grab us another round."

He ignored our objections and left for the bar. Awkwardly, Sotiny and I sat in the booth.

"Why did you two arrive together?" I asked, leaning my arm against the back of the booth. Dancers performed in cages and fire was blown in either direction. It was like a carnival in a bar. And yet, I was feeling anything but thrilled.

"Why does it matter?" she snipped. "I could ask the same of you and your two pretty twins. Another rendezvous, a one-night stand because that's all you can handle, right?"

"At least I can handle at least a one-night stand, little virgin." I regretted the words the moment they left my mouth. Her sharp penetrating glare pinned me like a bolt of lightning.

She shrugged off her long cream coat, revealing a low plunging black dress. A small pearl necklace adorned her throat, a few droplets gliding down and in between her breasts. My jaw clenched, the thought of how perfectly her breasts would fill my hands tormenting me. I looked away, far too tempted than I should ever be. "Do you really still think I'm a little virgin after moving to Manhattan?" she sneered.

Yes.

"And we met at the front, if you must know," she said, waving down Damon and Clover to our booth.

"Sorry we got stuck in traffic," Clover said exasperatedly as Damon took off her coat and pressed a kiss to her cheek. Sotiny and I shared a glance. Apparently outside of work he was claiming her indefinitely in front of Hayden.

"Has Hayden arrived yet?" Clover asked. I pointed to the bar where he was chatting up the bartender. I was almost envious that wasn't me. Not because I particularly fancied the bartender but at least it wasn't shrouded with this toxic tension. "I heard the negotiations went well."

"They did." I charmed a smile. "I told you we'd be out celebrating."

The waitress headed over to our table, placing two whiskeys and a pina colada down.

Sotiny defiantly grabbed another glass of whiskey, snubbing the pina colada. She winced as she took a mouthful. Fine. If she wanted to play that game tonight, be my guest. But I knew she'd come to regret it.

Chapter 5

Sotiny

My hips swayed to the beat in the club two levels down. I couldn't even remember the last time I'd been in a club, let alone so drunk. The whisky sloshed around in my glass as I moved to the music. I recalled that I enjoyed dancing as a child. "Wasted time" my mother had always told me, and I'd never made the time in my early twenties to go out with college acquaintances. Not when their only ambition was finding a guy for the night. I'm sure they'd be horrified if they'd learnt I was thirty-one and still very single. But I hadn't worked my ass off, working numerous jobs, to get to Harvard to focus on guys. Not that it helped me when I left Harvard anyway. I took a swig, downing the

30

unpleasant reminders along with the unpleasant taste.

Alex caught me. "You know it's kind of funny." I giggled out loud thinking about how much my single-hood spited even my mother. That the perfect little daughter she'd tried to raise and hated so fiercely, didn't depend on numerous men to get her by, unlike her.

"What's so funny?" Alex asked. He'd been watching me all night as I danced, the whisky running straight to my head. Damon and Clover had since left. And I had no idea what happened to Hayden but assumed he'd found himself some company for the night. After all, that's what men like that did, right? Just like the one holding me now. "I think you need some water, Sotiny."

I laughed. "Why? I'm having so much fun!" I said, lifting his hand so he could spin me under his arm. His expression softened as he watched me. I let go, swaying again to the beat, eyes closed and enjoying the pulse around me. The night was alive and my skin was sweaty from the heat.

"Stay here, I'm getting you some water," I heard Alex say amongst the beat of the music. When I felt a hand clasp around my waist, I expected it to be Alex. Instead, it was a man I'd never seen before.

"Hey, girlie, you look like you're having a good time," he said in a thick Boston accent. I pulled out of his grip, a cold sweat washing over me.

"I was having a better time before you came and interrupted me."

"Now that's not very nice," he flirted. The moment I stopped dancing, the room began to sway around me.

Oh shit. I think I'm going to be sick. Where was the exit? Lights sprinkled around me and people shoved back and forth, cold dread sinking in.

"You don't look so good. Maybe I should take you out for some fresh—"

Without control, I vomited, some of it splattering on his shoes.

"What the fuck?!" he yelled, pushing me out of his way.

With lightning speed, I fell into Alex's arms as he steadied me, then right hooked the guy. The man stumbled into a group of people.

"Alex!" I screamed. And then another wave of nausea hit me. He sized up the guy, but I clung to him pathetically. "Alex," I said quieter, completely forgetting about the man whose shoes I'd just vomited on. "I'm going to be sick."

Despite his obvious rage, he glanced at me and

ushered me through the crowd with a bottle of water in hand.

A bouncer ran up beside us and Alex waved him off. "Yea, yea, I know, I'm getting her out of here. And he shouldn't have touched or shoved her. Now get the fuck out of my way." I hadn't seen Alex lose his cool like this since... we were teenagers.

"Alex," one of the bartenders called out, pointing to a side exit. The moment he pulled me into the fresh air and it hit me like an ice-cold blanket, I barfed behind an overfilled trash can. All that whisky burned the same way up as it had going down. Alex brushed back parts of my hair, holding it out of the way as I sobbed pathetically with shaky hands.

"This is why I told you not to drink whiskey," he said rubbing my back.

"Are you fucking kidding me right now?" I growled.

He chuckled. "I love it when you use your potty mouth, Miss Granger."

"Don't call me—" Another hurl of vomit. I pressed a hand against the wall, bracing myself as I dry heaved. The freezing weather suddenly crept up on me and I shuddered, irritated. "My coat," I grumbled.

"We're not getting back in there tonight." His

leather jacket encompassed my shoulders. "Here." And then he gave me the bottled water.

"You shouldn't have punched him," I reprimanded groggily.

"He shouldn't have pushed you."

I swished water in my mouth and spat it onto the ground. "I vomited on his shoes."

"They were ugly shoes anyway," Alex scoffed. I sank further into my shoulders. "Doesn't this take you back?"

With a swirl of irritation and nostalgic memories I'd tried to forget, it had taken me back.

"I want to go home," I grumbled, still wobbly. I straightened and immediately slumped against him.

"Wooo there. I'll get you home safely. I've gotcha, baby girl."

A dizzy spell washed over me, quickly followed by complete darkness with the lingering oath that I'd never touch whiskey again.

Chapter 6

Alex
Age 17

It hadn't taken me long to find her. I sent her brother a text to let him know I'd found her and I'd bring her home. She was dangling on a swing, her back hunched over as she idly swayed from side to side. The park was dimly lit around her and no matter how defiant, a fifteen-year-old shouldn't have been sitting out here by herself.

"How'd you know I'd be here?" Sotiny asked, without turning around. The more reasonable question was *how did you know it was me?*

"Call it instinct," I said in a low tone matching hers. I pushed her ever so slightly, the size of my hand filling the middle of her back. She'd always been so petite and fragile looking.

"What happened, Sots?" I asked. A noticeable

tension immediately rippled through her. There would be consequence to what she'd done. She'd been raised in a way where she was expected to be nothing other than perfect. Where her mother was overbearingly harsh on her, that didn't extend to her brother, Tyson. And although he was my best friend and I lived next door, I had concerns for how they were individually treated.

Tyson and I were allowed out at parties and his mother would supply us booze even though neither of us were legal age and Sots wasn't even so much as allowed a sleepover. No boys. No weekends away. She was to silently live in the house under her mother's watchful gaze.

Sotiny was trained to be a doll around others, silent and well presented, smoothed over and perfect and finally, she'd snapped. I couldn't have been any prouder. "Sotiny?" I prompted again.

A heavy breath rippled out of her. "Mom's going to be angry."

"Yea she's pretty pissed," I laughed, thinking of her expression when she'd found out what Sotiny had done. Her feet dragged along the ground as she stared over her shoulder at me in disbelief.

"Why are you laughing?" she asked seriously. It was, after all, her who'd get in trouble but I found amusement in when people's tempers finally snapped. When everyone played the role of "perfect house" and something so slight unraveled them. That's when you saw their true nature. Just like Sotiny's.

"Well, I mean, your mother does look like a tomato when she gets angry. It looks like she's going to explode."

She considered this for a moment, all seriousness wrapped in her frail form. Those intelligent eyes came to a conclusion. She was smarter than what any of them realized. "She does, doesn't she?"

I agreed. "Are you going to tell me what really happened? Because everyone's already heard Tiffany's side of the story."

She tsked and began biting her thumbnail. With no one else around, she was herself, this vile little creature with a temperament. The version of her I liked the most. She had a voice and an opinion.

"She started rumors I was trying to steal her boyfriend and as if I'd ever try to touch that mohawk-wearing daft fool. And I have nothing against the mohawk but at least choose one color. But if you want multiple colors that's fine, just make sure you maintain it. But also, there's a school policy and I have no idea how he's allowed in with it. And also, he's a nitwit and treats her like absolute crap. Not to forget to mention I spotted him making out with Claurice who is supposed to be her friend. And then Claurice started saying I was the one who was kissing him behind Tiffany's back and then they all started yelling at me. And Claurice shoved me and said I was nothing but a petite and frail doll and I punched her... straight in the face."

I erupted in laughter. That was the funniest thing I'd heard all day. "Right in the face, huh?" I licked around my teeth, trying to calm my raging humor. She blushed and looked away. I'd noticed her reaction to my smile for a while now. Perhaps a little crush. I found something in it soothing but never delved deeper. I wasn't allowed to reciprocate something so sweet. Her brother had sworn she was off-limits. The moment she'd begun to develop, he'd sworn all of his friends off. *Especially me.*

"Sounds like Claurice deserved a smack in the face. And hey at least it wasn't in school so you won't have to worry about suspension."

She winced at that, the sudden consequence dawning on her. She looked down at her hand and that was when I noticed the slight bruising. She hadn't broken Claurice's nose, although in my opinion she probably deserved it.

I stepped around and knelt down, grabbing her hand. "How bad is it?" In the dim lighting, I couldn't see too well but I knew it wasn't bad enough that she needed to go to hospital. "It just needs some ice."

"Aren't you going to say you're disappointed or something?" she quietly asked.

I tried to hide my smirk. Who was I to judge anyone for getting into fights? I'd been called "meddlesome" for as long as I could remember and then when I started getting bigger than the bullies, everything changed. But Sotiny was different, she wasn't a complete asshole like me and the guilt of her own short fuse exploding was probably eating her alive. "I'm not disappointed. As long as you're okay and Claurice probably deserved it."

"Don't you think I'm in the wrong?" she asked again, so quick to expect reprimand and consequence.

"I'm not your mother, Sotiny, I'm not going lecture you on right or wrong. Only you can decide that for yourself."

She stared at me, that cold calculated gaze terrifying for most, especially when she came in such a small package. Coming in at only five foot five, she put most boys to their knees. She didn't need Tyson or me to keep them at a distance for her, that steely gaze and resolve was enough. It was completely different to how "inviting" her mother was, though I'd never mention the comparison out loud.

"Is Claurice okay?" she asked softly. I gently rubbed over the bruising, fixated on her tiny hand in mine. I wished for once, she'd only care about herself.

"I don't know, I never saw her," I honestly replied, looking up into that cold distant stare that resembled the depths of any dark ocean, but in the light and during the day, they were like a raging storm.

"Didn't you say everyone heard her side of the story?" Her gaze narrowed suspiciously.

"They did. I didn't. I started looking for you the moment they said you'd done a runner. I don't need to hear her side, Sots, because I believe you and that's that."

Slowly she pulled her hand out of mine. "You always make everything sound so easy."

"It's only people's pride and emotions that complicate everything."

She laughed and pushed off me, creating a slight sway of the swing. "He's a philosopher now."

I rarely admitted it to myself but I liked it when we had these moments alone. This was a side no one else saw. A side where Sotiny smiled for herself, not because she was told to or had to act a certain way. And I could never admit to myself or Tyson that I had a thing for the girl. I'd heard his warning loud and clear.

"Push me a little before I go home and am grounded for eternity, will you?" she demanded. That minor, bratty but selfish part of her coming out. Obliging and wishing we had a little longer, I did. Because I knew she wasn't kidding, her mother would make her life a living hell for the next few months and there was nothing I could do about it. At most, I could just ensure I stayed close and make sure it didn't get too out of hand.

Chapter 7

Sotiny

My head pounded, the tiny sliver of light coming through the window in my apartment the bane of my existence. I grumbled, my hand reaching for my cell in attempt to smack the alarm off. "Why?" I cried out loud. The bright screen lit my face and I moaned. Why did I ever think yoga was a good idea on a Saturday morning? Oh, that's right, because I never went out on a Friday night.

I muttered incoherently again under my breath as I narrowed my gaze on the small slither of light that passed through the blinds. Considering how much I heaved yesterday, I shouldn't have felt this worse for wear.

Beside my bed on the nightstand was a glass of

water and two painkillers. Without question, I downed them. I sat upright contemplating my existence and how embarrassingly messy I'd gotten last night, recalling patches of the events.

I pressed a hand to my stomach realizing I'd been changed into a loose-fitting shirt. How did I get home?

"Don't worry, I didn't look," Alex said by way of greeting as he opened my bedroom door. "Sotiny, how on earth can you live in this pigsty? There's crap everywhere."

"What are you doing in my apartment?"

"Is that what we're calling this space now? Because I just spent the last two hours piling things, throwing out random wrappers and do you really need that many editions of *Harry Potter* and *Star Wars*?"

I placed the glass back down on my bedside table. "Perhaps I hadn't made myself clear enough. *What* are you doing here?" Last night aroused so many other memories. Especially another drunken night we'd spent together from what felt like a lifetime ago. "What happened last night?" I said self-consciously, covering myself with the sweat-drenched blankets. Why was everything so fuzzy?

"Don't worry your virginity's still intact, if that's what you're implying."

"Will you stop saying that," I snapped, infuriated he was in my home making jokes. I never invited him here. This was supposed to be my space. My home. And just because I'd been reckless and had too many drinks, he thought he could permit himself into the one place where he couldn't bombard me. Heat radiated my cheeks.

My head felt like it was spinning. Oh God, had I made a fool of myself last night? Did the others see? I shouldn't have drunk the whisky. What will they think of me now? Will I be fired? Did I disgust them? Did I say or do something wrong?

"Sotiny? I asked how's your head?" Alex asked, ignoring my outburst. Why was he always like this? He'd taunted me to no end and then when I hated him most, he'd pretend to care.

"Why do you even care?" I asked begrudgingly. "What because some guy tried to hit on me you think you have the right to come in as some prince charming?"

His eyes boggled. "Are you insane? You really think it's because some guy tried to hit on a drunk woman at the bar that I helped you get home safely?"

"A drunk woman? Oh, as in because if I were sober he wouldn't have tried?"

"Not with that bratty attitude of yours. Why do you always do this? As soon as we lay down the swords for one minute, you come back swinging with the most insane things. Stop trying to push me away."

"I'm not trying anything. Are you that dense? When I say I don't want anything to do with you, you clearly can't take a hint."

"What the actual fuck, Sotiny? I helped you last night. I didn't do anything wrong. I told you not to drink the whisky!"

"Oh because you're always right?"

He threw his hands up in the air. "Am I wrong right now? And that's certainly rich coming from *you*." His voice trembled with rage.

I knew he was right. He might've been a playboy but Alex wouldn't ever hurt a woman, let alone leave her alone and defenseless, especially as drunk as I was. And yet, I couldn't help it. I wanted him out. I wanted to push him as far away as possible. Alex was a complexity and toxicity I didn't want back in my life.

"I've never been your concern. So for the hundredth time. Leave me alone," I stated coldly.

"Not my problem?" he huffed. "You're my fucking *wife*."

I was all fangs again. "Don't call me that. Don't you dare have the audacity to call me that!" I grabbed the glass and threw it at the wall beside him. Glass shattered everywhere. I hoped it scared him off. The mere thought and complexity of him saying it out now forced me to boiling point.

"You're unbelievable you know that?! That ugly side of you is rearing its head and you don't know how to cover it up anymore. That's not on me, baby girl. That's all you!"

I ignored him, trying my hardest to rein in this furious rage within me that wanted to scream, punch, bite, and explode.

"Fuck this, I don't need this today."

When the front door slammed behind him, I grabbed my pillow and screamed into it. Did he feel obliged and chained to me because of my brother? Was it really hard to keep the past in the past? The past twelve months had been the greatest opportunity for my career but it's my own living hell having to face Alex almost every day again.

My cell began to buzz, my mother's name lighting the screen. That was a hard pass. With wobbly legs, I stepped over the broken glass and toward my en suite for a shower. Not before peering into my small kitchenette and living room. Alex really had cleaned it spotless. On the bench, two vanilla cupcakes were plastic-wrapped.

I felt my steely resolve glaze over like a calm balm. I could look after myself. I didn't need Alex in my life. And no matter how many times I tried to shove him away, he just kept crawling back, almost addicted to the same internal suffering that I felt like I deserved. I just needed to be alone and for some reason, he couldn't take a hint.

Chapter 8

Sotiny

Begrudgingly, because Alex had commented on the state of my apartment it'd been immaculate ever since. And was it even a matter of choice or question that I needed that many copies of *Harry Potter* and *Star Wars*? Was he out of his mind? Of course I did.

A light sprinkle of snow had begun to line the streets of New York. When I finished my early morning Monday yoga class, I felt much calmer. Friday night and drinking had been an abnormality for me and now I remembered why. I never made great decisions when I'd had too many drinks. And I might've not drunk myself to oblivion if I'd been able to keep my anger in check instead of being so infuriated by Alex's playboy ways. And what infuriated me even more was that he was all I could think about.

"Sotiny!" The instructor from my yoga class called out from behind. I swirled around plastering a polite smile. "We were worried about you, you didn't show up on Saturday. You've never missed a class. Is everything okay?" My smile wavered.

"Yes, everything's fine. I've just had a lot of things on since my boss has been ill the last few weeks. But nothing to concern yourself with. I won't miss it again, sorry."

She chuckled. "You don't have to apologize. People skip out all the time. Hell, so do I sometimes. But in the twelve months that you've been here I've never seen *you* skip once, so just wanted to check in and make sure everything's okay."

Was my routine that predictable? Then again, I knew it was. Same times. Same days. My schedule was always very particular.

"We're inviting some of our fellow yogis for a little Christmas get together here at the studio if you'd like to join. An email's being sent out next month. I know it's still two months away, but we like to give everyone plenty of notice."

"I'll consider it." Although I had no intention of going. I didn't need friends and I didn't have the time to slot anyone or any other activity in. "Thank you for the invitation. I'll see you tomorrow, okay?" I grabbed a raspberry-flavored water from the fridge and raised it to Lucy, the receptionist, so she could add it to my account.

With the studio being only two blocks from my apartment, it offered me plenty of time to shower at home and be at the café near work right on schedule.

The same barista from last week served me again. "Good morning, Sotiny, the same?"

"Yes please."

"Michelle's back," her boss called out from the side. Regine was a woman in her mid-forties with bright red hair and freckles plastered across her face. "She was here only ten minutes before you crept in. She's looking well."

"That's good to hear," I said, feeling relieved to know she'd be back in the office again. I had a few notes I wanted to run over with her, and although I often preferred emails with most, I did enjoy Michelle's company. The doorbell rang as someone entered.

"Oh, I put full cream milk in, is that okay?" the barista asked me. I internally grimaced. I didn't want to make a big deal though. I didn't want her thinking

I was particular or I watched my calories or something of the sorts. "That's okay," I lied.

"It's not," Alex said, not looking in my direction. I hadn't even noticed him walking in. "If it's not skim she won't drink it. It'll sit at her desk all day. And just the usual for me."

I went to argue but said nothing when his wide back blocked me out of the way and he greeted the barista with a smile. "That's no problem at all. You two seem to know one another well."

"Not particularly," Alex charmed. I could sense it in his tone and in the way that she blushed that he was back to his usual self. I noticed his lack of gym bag today. Often the mornings he skipped his boxing with Damon meant he wasn't at his house for the night. Another Manhattan woman bites the dust.

I decided to replicate his sentiment. Just go back to normal like nothing had happened. I searched through the side glass door admiring the snow, far more interested in the weather than Alex's love life.

"Your coffee's ready for you, Sotiny, sorry about the mix-up. It's skim now so you should have no problem," she beamed.

With a polite smile, I thanked her and left, relieved that Alex didn't try to start any small talk. After the weekend, I didn't know how to face him. I didn't want to. The last thing I heard as I made my leave was the new barista giggling at something he'd said.

The cold slap of air and snow was a nice wake-up call. Although I'd been considered frail as a child and caught colds quickly, I'd learned to enjoy its bitter nature as an adult.

As expected, no one else was in the office at this time. I stood outside Michelle's office door. Her effortless smile settling a calm over me. Although there was only eight years between us in age, she offered a no-nonsense demeanor, but wound up in that was a motherly supportive undertone.

Despite my lack of experience within the fields, she'd taken a risk to hire me and in a way, I felt as if she'd taken me under her wing and quickly exploited my strengths as her personal assistant. I was grateful to Michelle for giving me the opportunity I'd lacked when I'd finished at Harvard. It never looked good on a CV when five years had been wasted with a multitude of jobs instead of pursuing that career immediately. As a bonus, Manhattan was a huge distance from my hometown Fairhope, Alabama, taking away any risk that my mother would ever try to find me.

"Are you feeling any better? Have the doctors

figured out what's wrong?" It'd been weeks now she'd been ill without cause.

"Good morning, Sotiny," she chimed with a half-cocked smile. She carried herself in that hard demeanor I'd grown to respect. If there was a staple piece for "girl boss" to put up on the wall it was Michelle Brogardt. "Nothing yet. But I wanted to try and make it in and give Damon a few days off with Clover. My good days are far and few between when I'm not coiled around a toilet bowl."

"Are you sure you should be pushing yourself?" I asked as I sat at her desk, delightfully surprised by my first sip of the skim milk latte.

She laughed. "Pushing myself is all I know. If anything, I feel like old age and ailments are catching up with me *because* I've slowed down. And how have you been finding it? From what I can see you've kept everything running smoothly while I've been gone, which I'm grateful for. I'd be lost without you."

"I have a good mentor."

She scoffed. "You never needed my mentorship, you came as a package deal yourself. I hope you'll find confidence in that soon."

I kept my expression calm, although I was confused. Did I not come across as confident despite my efforts?

"I see the contract went well with onboarding Hayden Zilch and we're going ahead with the sports magazine which is a huge accomplishment. Although I knew setting you on the project would ensure a win."

She sipped on her green tea, leaning back in the chair comfortably. Her long black glossy hair was tied into a high ponytail that caught the shimmer of the light outside in the hall.

"I'm pleased to say it did."

"Anything else I should know on the matter?" she asked cryptically. I could feel the blood drain from my face. Had she heard something about the weekend? Had I embarrassed myself? Was I going to lose my job for showing such a hideous side? "How have you and Alex been working together on this project?"

"Alex?" I asked, confused by what he had to do with anything.

"Yes Alex, you two are still working on the project together, aren't you?"

"Of course. Yes fine."

"I was just curious, you two have always held a bit of tension I wanted to know if you've learnt to work together more efficiently?"

I ignored the urge to bite my thumbnail. What

was she suggesting? Had the others in the office found out about our history? But the only other person who knew about our *relationship* was Alex.

"We're working just fine together, I think," I added, unsure. What answer was she wanting from me?

"You think?" she pressed, raising one singular brow. A small smirk twisted her features. It was her, after all, who'd purposefully assigned us on this project together. I was aware everyone in the office had a reasonably close relationship with Alex, *including* the Brogardt family by way of Damon and him being such good friends. Had he said something?

"Then that's good," she said, sifting through a few papers. "Because Hayden Zilch has requested a small team join him for a week in Ithaca to start working on the media and spread. He also has one of his all-star football players raising funds for charity before the new season starts. I need you and Alex to build a relationship with Hayden's team that he'll be boarding onto this project as well and make sure the interviews are executed perfectly."

"A week?" I squeaked. One week stuck with Alex Fields after I threw a glass at him to chase him out of my home sounds outstandingly delightful.

"Does that interfere with any personal plans? It's all paid for, of course."

"That's fine." My fingers curled over my laptop bag resting on my lap. "And when will this be?"

"Starting next week. I know it's short notice, but we'd be grateful if you can be on the frontline for it."

"Of course," I said with a polite smile. And although I was grateful for the time away and an all-expenses-paid trip, I wasn't however prepared to spend an entire week with Alex. This was making it excruciatingly difficult to avoid him.

Chapter 9

Alex

Smack. I punched into the handheld pad. Damon shook it off.

"You do remember that pad is attached to my hand?" he remarked, repositioning. I bounced back and forth. I could feel the heat rising alongside the tension in my body. I rolled out my arm and shoulder. "Why so tense today?"

"No particular reason," I lied, smacking against the two hand pads.

"For the decade I've known you, Alex, it takes a bit to get under your skin. You're one of the easiest, go with the flow, wind up everyone else with tongue in cheek kind of guy I know." *If only he'd seen my temper when I was younger.* "And I'm telling you, I've never seen you strung up like this." He gave me that stare—the one that often demanded an answer, especially without him asking twice. But our relationship had never been like that. Or more importantly and expectantly, I never bowed down to his family name. "Would it serve you well if I reminded you that I was your boss?"

"You're my what now?" I said, punching into the pads and making him step back.

He charmed an arrogant smile. "Could it be that a certain little miss has gotten under Alex's skin?"

"My beautiful, glistening, perspired skin," I correct as I rolled a hand down my abs. "And don't be ridiculous. I just don't understand why two of us would have to go to Ithaca? I can do it myself, or hell she's more than capable to do it on her own."

"I never deliberated on any one woman, Alex." Damon seemed smug. "But that's right, she who should not be named." If only he knew the complications involved when it came to Sotiny Bryer.

I stood tall, assessing him. "Careful you're starting to sound more and more like Clover every day."

"And you're starting to sound like a madman," Damon accused. "What is it really between you two? Did she refuse you on a one-night stand?"

I flicked my wrist straps off, my temper rising by the conversation. No, I had to keep my cool.

"There's nothing between us," I huffed. It might've been fun for him, innocent even, but there was a dark well he was forcing us to both look down. One that I was certain Sotiny and I never wanted to look into again. And I couldn't blame Damon for jabbing; I'd do the same to him.

"Well, that's certainly not what it looks like. It was with your recommendation during the recruiting process we hired Sotiny. And she has not disappointed but if this is going to interfere with the contract with Hayden Zilch and our sports edition than I need to know if there's a problem?"

"I don't have a problem. I mean don't you have a problem?"

"Excuse me?" His gaze narrowed. "Watch your next words carefully, Alex."

"You were the one getting jealous over your girlfriend's old university friend reunion. Is that going to affect the contract?"

"No, because I know how to rein my temperament in," he growled carefully. "Unlike some."

I casually raised my hands in the air as if in defeat. "You're right. I'm sorry. I just, I just have a bit on lately. I'm sorry I didn't mean to take it out on you."

"You promise me this isn't going to be a problem?"

"Not a problem at all," I said sincerely, hoping to convince him. "And don't be so upset I'm kicking your ass out in the ring. Maybe you're getting too comfortable in your relationship status."

Although he was wearing a shirt, Damon looked down at his chiselled physique affronted. "Are you implying I'm getting fat?"

"I don't know, Mr. Brogardt, are you getting cushy in love?"

"Get your ass back into this ring right now," he demanded. I laughed heading for the showers.

"I already know when I'm not going to win a fight so no thank you." I laughed, feeling lighter after the round. I'd discovered this boxing gym the very first day I landed in New York and I'd been a member ever since. There was something nice about having a sparring partner, especially when it was your boss.

Chapter 10

Sotiny

When I'd inquired about Clover's hometown of Ithaca, she wrote down an extensive list of cafes and bars to check out. The university city was only a four-hour drive from Manhattan. Not that I minded the drive, it was simply stuck on the road with Alex for any length of time that irked me. But I reminded myself that this job meant more to me than any tension and history we shared. He drove his car, some kind of sports car that no doubt was purchased to impress all his lady friends. Last I'd seen, before he'd moved to New York, he had an old beaten-up truck that his father owned. Who knows what's happened to it since.

Despite a few channel changes on the radio, I

was able to read my book in peace. Whenever I had spare time, I always read recent releases in the Young Adult charts, where my true passions and dreams lied. Literature.

It was late Sunday evening when Alex picked me up from my apartment. We had one week booked in a hotel in Ithaca and would be meeting with Simon, one of the journalists from the office, tomorrow—his time there was a few days shorter. And then on the weekend, Clover had insisted we join her and Damon for her mother's birthday before we drove back to Manhattan the following day.

A gritty clunk gave way beneath us, startling me out of my trance in an action-packed part.

"What was that?" I asked.

Alex seemed flustered as he looked over the steering wheel. "I don't know, give me a second," he said, pulling over the side of the road. I'd since learnt he owned a Mustang GT. Whatever that meant. I'd hoped the car would be invincible considering it certainly looked like it. "I need to check under the hood."

"The hood? Why what's wrong with it?" I inquired, stepping out of the car with him. It was freezing. We parked on the side of the thin gravelly road. We were in the middle of nowhere, nothing but fields to be seen on either side.

Alex lifted the hood and smoke billowed out. "That's not good," I told him.

He gave me an effective glare. "You think I don't know that?"

I shrugged. Sure, he and my brother used to play around with cars in their teens but it didn't count toward either of them knowing what they were actually doing. I just thought they were crazed after watching *the Fast and the Furious*.

"You can sit back in the car, I'll check this out."

"Do you know what you're doing?" I inquired, arms folded.

"Sotiny," he growled. I raised my hands defensively.

"Fine but I have a bad feeling about this," I admitted. I shrugged my coat on and sat back inside flicking through the final pages of the chapter. A few minutes later, I leaned my back against the car. As much as I was enjoying the silence, I certainly didn't want a stalemate in the middle of nowhere.

Thirty minutes passed, and inspector Alex, the not-qualified mechanic, still made no progress. The sun was beginning to set and the ice chill of the night began to descend. Despite having my coat on it was still slipping through and we still hadn't seen another car since.

I checked my cell, we were still in SOS.

"Alex, you're going to catch a cold out here," I said. He was only wearing that stupid fitted shirt that showed far too much of his physique than I'd like to admit. "At least put your jacket on."

He remained silent, tinkering away with whatever contraption he found in the boot of his car.

I certainly didn't want to be stuck out here before nightfall. "When I was studying the GPS prior to us leaving, if my calculations are correct by the signs we've gone past, I think there's a motel about two miles up."

Alex's dark-green gaze fixed on me. It was like looking into a forest of pine trees with no end. Only depth and life sparked from within.

"You studied the GPS map?" he asked disbelieving.

"Well of course I did," I said, affronted. Especially for situations just like this.

Alex whistled, shaking his head. "You're one hell of a woman you know that?"

My heart fluttered, followed by the sharp sting and infliction of any of his compliments or sweet words. A reminder and automated response when

Alex Fields was around. That and he was most certainly mocking me.

Alex looked at his car, then into the distance, then back at his car.

"Alex, I swear if you make me freeze my ass off out here because your pride is getting in the way and you don't want to leave your bedazzled car on the side of the road..."

"I get it," he said, raising his hands. Cold puffs escaped his lips. "It's cold out here isn't it?"

I held his coat in the air. *How many times had I told him to put this on?*

Circumstantially, I wanted to scream but a lot was riding on this trip. I didn't want to disappoint Michelle. I wasn't going to ruin it by having another outburst at Alex. I grabbed my toothbrush, tooth-paste and floss out of my suitcase in the trunk of his car.

"Really? You'll leave everything else behind but that?" he inquired. "We're going to get the car towed and head into town. You realize that right?"

"I'd rather not leave anything to chance, Alex. If we get stranded in some dodgy hotel be damned I'm not going to be able to at least have clean teeth. And despite the unfitting circumstances of having to wear these boots"—I pointed the cream boots for effect—

"for the next two miles, I refuse to complain. But I *also* refuse to go to sleep with my teeth unbrushed and flossed."

"I hope your calculations are correct and we don't have to walk three miles," he goaded. I slammed the boot shut offering him an ice-cold stare. "You know in those boots and all. And we'll be fine. We'll get a lift into town."

"Ha. Ha. Very funny. Don't even dare ask to share my toothpaste if we are stranded."

"It's a hotel, surely they'll have toothpaste," he shrugged, glancing over his car one last time like a lovestruck puppy.

"Famous last words, my friend. Now hurry up. I'm freezing," I adjusted my coat and threw on a beanie. Nothing could ever go right when around Alex Fields, and I wasn't leaving anything to chance.

Chapter 11

Sotiny

My fingertips felt like ice by the time we'd finally arrived at the hotel. A small flickering light illuminated that there was in fact vacancy. The half-hanging frame that read "Hotel" however, should be enough of a deterrent for most.

We peered up at the sign. My arms were crossed and Alex's mouth was agape.

"Sotiny, we're not going to be stuck here. It'll be fine," he began.

"Well I hope so because I'm tired and hungry."

"You're *hungry*? What are you going to do out here *hunt*?"

I scoffed and beelined for the reception. "Since

when did you become such a princess? The city life has really gotten to you, hasn't it?"

"The what? Are you calling me soft?" he asked, storming after me, his ego more offended now than the thought of staying in this motel.

"I don't know, have you become accustomed to the silk pillows you lay on every night, Mr. Fields?"

"How did you know my pillowcases were silk?" he asked.

I rolled my eyes. "It was a guess. But not surprised."

The small doorbell rang as I entered, the windows dusty and barely able to see through.

An older woman with a cigarette hanging out of her mouth looked up from the magazine she was flicking through.

"Hi, our car broke down about two miles out. We were hoping we might be able to call for someone to tow it into town," I said politely. She looked me up and down with a sneer, and then her glazed gray eyes landed on jackpot when she saw Alex.

"Ain't nobody going to come out at this time," she crooned.

I exchanged an awkward glance with Alex, near wanting to push him forward as tribute. He was so good running his mouth with the ladies, he might as well prove his worth now.

"There's no way at all we could possibly call someone out to have it towed?" he asked sheepishly.

"Sorry, sugar, as much as I'd like to help you out, no can do. But we should be able to organize something early in the morning. I could call in a favor for you. But you might have to hold up here for the night."

Alex glanced begrudgingly my way. *Princess.*

"Are we possibly able to call a cab to come and pick us up?" he asked.

A coarse cough ran through her as she laughed. "At this time? Sorry, sugar, you'll be waiting for that lift with the tow truck tomorrow."

The color drained from his face. Smug, enjoying Alex's discomfort, I held two fingers up. "Can we please get two separate rooms?"

The lady started laughing again, a coarse cough following. "Sorry, sugar, I only got one double bedroom."

It was time for the blood to drain from my face.

"That's very generous," Alex quickly said. "Of course, we'd love to, right?" His expression was too elated. He was enjoying this far too much as he handed over his card. "I mean we don't have any other choice. We'll have to wait until morning. And do you by chance have any sort of meals, the little one here is *starving*."

The woman inspected me with a light undignified snort. I offered a curt smile.

"We've got some cereal and some crisps. I can even lend you some milk," she suggested.

"When you say lend?"

"Sotiny," Alex growled in warning. "Go on, choose some crisps," he encouraged. "You can have more than one packet. I know how hungry you are."

I couldn't exaggerate the smile any further. With a brief glance over the selection, I grabbed two of each flavor. He blazingly stared at me as I bundled the eight packets in my arms. I grabbed four salami sticks and six chocolate bars. Before my hands couldn't possibly fit any more in, for added measure, I grabbed a Twinkie in my mouth.

"You're not seriously going to eat that," Alex growled.

"Yes, I am," I muffled around the Twinkie.

"You sure can pack it away, little lady," the woman said. "And what about you, handsome, you going to grab anything for yourself?" she asked, blowing smoke into his face.

His gaze flashed to me, offended by the mere

stench of the place. I offered an exaggerated smile. "No" was all he said as he paid the very reasonable and affordable price.

With a tiny key and numbered keyring the size of Alex's hand, he stepped back out into the cold. The sun had now completely vanished. "Number three," he said out loud. There were only six rooms to choose from, all of which were closed with curtains drawn.

He slipped the key into the lock, wriggling it a few times. When it didn't open, he shoulder barged it, almost falling through as it finally gave way with a loud thud.

I tried not to openly laugh at his short curse as he turned on the light and stared at the small room. I pushed around him taking in all its glory, which was an overstatement. Paint peeled off the wall, stains on the carpet with threadbare curtains. The only thing adjacent the double bed was a small TV on the wall and two sofas. A door led into a small shower and toilet.

"We're going to get eaten alive by rats tonight, you do realize that, don't you?" he said begrudgingly.

I shrugged, placing all my goodies at the end of the bed. In all fairness, it was a hellhole. "I think it's charming."

His eyebrows knitted together. "You really don't want me to survive the night, do you?"

"Oh stop being a sook," I said, walking over to the heater. It was, however, cold in here. "And if I didn't want you making it through the night, I would've dealt with that myself years ago."

A sombre silence. My devilish smile curved. I clicked the heater over... but nothing happened. It was turned on at the wall. I clicked it over again. Nothing.

"Let me have a look at it," Alex said, leaning over.

"Much like how you looked at your car?" I asked folding my arms over my knees. He offered me an effective side glance.

Uncomfortable by his cologne that filled my entire being, I shuffled to the side. After a few mutters and curse words, he looked at me deadpanned.

"What do your calculations look like in miles walking from here to Ithaca?"

I gave him another brooding and effective glare. With a light chuckle, his muscled and hunched figure stretched out. "We can't sleep in here like this. I'll see if they have some kind of portable heater."

That only left one unaddressed crisis in the

room. I glanced toward the bed. There was no way we were both sleeping on there together.

"It's okay, Miss Granger, you can have the bed. I'll sleep on the couch."

It couldn't even be classed as a couch; it was a small framed chair with barely any padding.

"Now go and have a shower, it might warm you up a bit, and besides—" He stretched his hand out toward my hair and I automatically resisted the urge to lean in, instead putting distance between us. Defiantly, he pulled something from my hair and assessed it. "—you have a few bugs in your hair you might want to wash out."

"What?!" I stuttered, combing my fingers through my hair.

He began laughing as I grabbed his hand and opened it to reveal an empty palm. He flicked my nose with his other hand. "That's payback for all these snacks you're not going to eat."

I crossed my arms over my chest. "You don't know that." Defiantly, I grabbed a salami stick and ripped it open with my teeth. A brief flash of heated tension rolled off Alex, his attention drawn to my lips. I lost my breath, my body feeling that unnatural heated warmth on the few times he'd looked at me like that. Pushing away old memories, I bit into the meaty stick. "Delicious."

Alex chuckled to himself and waved me off. "Have a shower, Sots. You get sick easily and we've been outside for the last hour. Surely, they'll have some soap in this forsaken place."

And with that, he was gone.

Chapter 12

Alex

The moment her teeth sank into that wrapper it reminded me of our night in Vegas. When she'd efficiently and desperately ripped away the corner of the condom wrapper. I tried my hardest to block out those memories but found myself staggering around the corner of the building instead. If I thought about it anymore, I'd get a hard on.

But I'd thought about that night so many times over the years. How I'd play it out differently. How I fantasised about throwing her light weight around and claiming every inch. Those intelligent eyes that missed nothing, always attentive and would no doubt be attentive to my needs as I would be hers. That turned down smile and scornful stare when she wasn't pretending to be someone else. Pretending to be what her mother conditioned her to be.

I kicked off the wall. History. We had too much damn history for me to ever survive a night like this. In the car for the first two hours of the drive, sitting so close to her was hard enough. Her floral scent of jasmine swirled around in my car, soaking into every part of the fabric. She was driving me mad. No matter how much I wanted to hate her and stay away. I never could, even though she hated every part of me. That was a reality I had to live with.

Despite my efforts and charm, the receptionist had nothing to offer besides a small pedestal heater. She didn't seem surprised when I told her the heater was broken even when she boldly stated, "How surprising, that's new."

By the time I'd returned, Sotiny was under the blankets in the bed with her jacket over top as an extra layer. She was elbow deep in a packet of the crisps, assessing both sides of flavoring before putting it into her mouth. And if memory served correctly, she always sucked the flavoring off first. The mere thought taking me to another fantasy entirely.

She tried to talk around her mouthful, the words incoherent.

"Sotiny... not with your mouth full." I gave

her an effective glare. This little wild thing, all messy-haired and makeup-free as best as she could with a small smudge of mascara beneath her eyes. This was the real Sotiny. The one I'd fallen for those many years ago and the same very creature that was caged by her own devices.

She swallowed. "What did she say?"

"She gave us a pedestal heater and another blanket." I indicated the single-sized blanket thrown over my shoulder. "And another packet of crisps in apology." I threw it at the end of the bed to add to her collection.

"Oooh goodie," she added as she assessed another crisp before eating it.

"Please don't tell me you're counting the calories on each and every crisp," I quipped as I installed the pedestal heater.

She scoffed. "Please, counting calories was never my thing. But more so your thing, my friend. Remember? Me need protein. Me man strong." I chuckled under my breath. She counted everything else. Why would calories be any different? But she did particularly love snacks, especially sweets. *Especially* vanilla cupcakes with buttercream. Not that her mother ever allowed her to enjoy such simple pleasures, which is why I used to sneak her the treats.

Now she was a full-grown woman but barely ever indulged. The low rumble of the heater began. But I wasn't very hopeful it'd be enough to keep the room warm for the night. The winter nights were freezing, and we were in the middle of nowhere. I searched around the walls questioning if they were even insulated.

"Relax, city boy, we'll be fine," she grumbled around a mouthful of crisps.

City boy? We both grew up in Fairhope, Alabama. Where my accent was completely diluted, she still had that certain charm about her. "Give me one of those," I said, reaching out my hand. She snatched the bag away, those panda eyes staring back at me with craziness.

"There's another eight packets on the end of the bed, have at it," she dryly cooed.

"But I want one out of that particular packet," I said pointedly.

"No," she huffed. "What about your protein intake, won't this jeopardize it," she said smugly, raising a crisp defiantly. We stared one another off and I leapt, reaching for the crisp.

"No!" she screamed trying to move it out of my

reach. I grabbed hold of her wrist and bit down on the crisp, pulling it out of her hand. "Alex!" She laughed. A genuine laugh, rumbling through her. It was contagious, as it always had been. *As she had always been.* Behind the armor and ice, lay this beautifully imperfect creature.

I stared into her icy blue gaze, our proximity dawning on both of us. Her breath hitched, her chest rose in the tight-fitting, cream, long-sleeved shirt. How many times had I thought about cupping those perfect hand-sized breasts? To kiss that scornful mouth? To be buried inside of her and have her scream out my name? Not in hate but in passionate demand. Before she could push me away, before she could spit vile and hateful words and retract into that shell of hers, I let go of her wrist and pushed off the bed.

I wanted nothing more than to hold her there, to position her beneath me. But like a frightened little rabbit, she'd find a way to escape. And I should know better than to try anything on her at all. "Thanks for sharing." I cockily smiled, looking over my shoulder. Her hand had dropped into her lap, a tension and complexity rolling over her features. It was the same every time. These feelings she tried to run away from. This distance she kept between us.

And sometimes I thought she genuinely hated me. But it was the glimpse of moments like these when without realizing it, she slipped into her genuine self, that I saw her. Saw the real her, happy and free, without limiting beliefs or expectations. But we were all fucked up in our own way. And I'd learnt not to push. Not when it came to Sotiny Bryer.

"I'm going to take a shower," I said, throwing off my jacket and pulling off my shirt. I laid it over the armchair near the pedestal heater. It'd gotten pretty cold when I hadn't worn my jacket to fix the car. And if I'd known we'd be stuck here, then I might've brought a spare change of clothes for both of us.

The shower at least offered a scorching heat. I stood with both hands against the tiles, letting the hot water wash over my back. And they had at least given us a free bar of soap. How long it'd been in here... who knew.

I stared down at my erect, thick, throbbing cock. What it wanted was little more than six feet away and yet it'd been the one thing I'd denied it all these years. No matter how many women... they never meant a damn thing. I wanted to stroke myself thinking of Sotiny but it wasn't my right to have. She'd outright rejected me time and time again. And no matter how much I yearned for her, it was a fantasy that wouldn't see the light of day.

I began to focus on the project, our reason for coming to Ithaca, and my poor fucking car. But despite this shitty run-down hotel, at least I was able to see her genuinely smile at least one more time. I internally growled. If Damon or someone heard me thinking like this, I'd be roasted. I dared to risk the soap, scrubbing myself of all these dead-end thoughts and deeply buried feelings.

The hot shower, not surprisingly, ran cold within a few minutes. I sighed, almost bemused by the state of the hotel. Though in fairness, what they charged was pretty appropriate for its state. The small square piece towel was barely a small stiff cloth to wrap around my waist.

I sighed to myself. Now she'd think I was trying to make a move on her if I waltzed out half dressed. Then again, I was already begging to freeze my ass off. "Sotiny, don't look I'm half naked."

She snorted over another crisp. "Do you really think you have something I haven't seen before?" she quipped. Her jaw tightened as her gaze raked down my body. She quickly focused on the snacks at her disposal. Within the short time I'd been gone, she'd already demolished most of the snacks. "Dry your hair or you'll catch a cold," she added as she found her book suddenly interesting again.

"Stress eating again?" I asked.

I could feel the eye roll without even looking in her direction. "I would hardly count four packets of crisps, three salami sticks and two chocolate bars, stress eating. It barely makes up for a proper meal."

I shook my head. Ah, her ever-logical reasoning for her food rationing once again when she decided to go all out on the snacks.

I could feel her gaze glued to me as I assessed my shirt; it was still slightly damp but better than nothing at all. Her gaze was burning into the small of my back. A male pride filled me; at least she was still slightly curious about my physique. That was progress, wasn't it?

Where I might've toyed with her slightly, I knew better than to comment. If she thought I didn't know she was watching me, then I'll let her believe it. Better that than her storming out of the room and choosing to die of frostbite than spend a night in here with me.

Back in the bathroom, I threw on my boxers and the shirt. I sighed at my grim state trying to at least comb through my hair. Light curls had begun to spring up from the damp moisture.

"This heater isn't doing anything at all, is it?" I rhetorically asked as I walked back out and checked over its functions.

"The best it can. And dry your hair," Sotiny instructed again as she sashayed past me with her toothbrush and toothpaste. I hated how right she was about the possibility of us being stuck here. And my teeth did feel pretty gross.

"Sotiny—"

Before I could even finish, she held out the toothpaste. "Tell me I was right first though."

I grimaced. "You were right. You always are." *Almost always.*

With a triumphant grin, she squirted a small piece onto my finger. We stood side by side, the small circular mirror the only other thing we could stare at, and yet we were stealing glances through it at one another. Her petite height didn't even come to my shoulders. It reminded me of when we were teenagers and I'd stay over at their house. How we'd silently brush our teeth beside one another, that slow burning tension and innocence building between us. Those unsaid thoughts and feelings overshadowed by the promise I'd made to her brother. She was completely off-limits. And yet, I'd still managed to fuck that up.

Gently, she spat into the sink, holding back her short strawberry-blonde hair. I'd remembered when it was a long and fiery red. The moment she turned eighteen, she changed it. Said it reminded her too much of her mother's, and so now she pointedly maintained it every four weeks, redoing the roots so no one could guess her natural color.

"Do you ever think you'll go back to your natural color?" I asked curiously.

Her gaze darted to mine, a dark storm swirling in those calculated blue eyes. "No."

With a slight flick of her wrist, she walked into the living room, no care for the wrappers that littered the floor. I sighed. When she was like this, she had no regard for what was around her. When she was stressed, she let everything fall apart, well except what everyone else might see.

I collected the packets around her. She grumbled under her breath. "I was going to pick those up in the morning."

I knew she would've. She'd always been either a complete clean freak or let it all go. It curled a warmth in my chest. How was it that only I knew this about her?

She'd curled herself into her blankets, sniffing and darting upright. "Something smells like smoke."

Sure enough, the small pedestal heater had begun to smoke. "You can't be serious," I said, kneeling in front of the small new device and now bane of my existence. "How bad could our luck possibly be?" I switched it off at the wall, a small spark offering its final protest until complete silence encompassed the room. "Fuck, I'm going straight to the reception and—"

"Alex, it's just one night. There's nothing we can do," Sotiny quietly said.

"We can't sleep in here, Sot's. You're going to freeze."

"We'll be fine," she protested.

I sank back into the small couch; I was certain a spring was digging into my ass. This day couldn't have possibly gone any worse.

"But that blanket's not going to be enough to keep you warm." I could barely make out her words. "You can sleep in here with me. Just don't get any bright ideas."

She curled further into herself as if to hide from what she just offered. A ripple tightened my jaw. How could I possibly share a bed with her *without* having any thoughts around it? And yet, I knew that by the morning the cold, sharp-edged Sotiny would be back. All confidence and work-obsession renewed.

"We don't have to—"

"It's fine, Alex, don't make a big deal about it," she blurted. It'd be only a week ago that she'd thrown a glass in my direction in thanks for helping her. And now she was offering to share the same bed. It was the same ping pong every time. Whenever she'd let me in, she'd just as quickly close off to me. And I was all the fool for taking whatever scraps she'd give me. And yet, she had every reason to punish me because I deserved it for what I'd done to her.

"Okay," I agreed. I threw the small single blanket over her. She couldn't have been further off the bed or she'd be curled over to the side. The bed protested under my weight, the soft mattress dipping as I turned my back to hers. It was warmer, if only slightly.

I could hear her heavy breathing, the very warmth of her somehow filling my lungs.

"You know I saw on a documentary once that in the wild and cold people remove their clothes and huddle closely because it makes them warmer," I educated her.

"Don't push it, Alex," she growled.

I chuckled, appreciating the small bite. I

might've been shit out of luck today, but it all made up for this moment. For her simply allowing me to be by her side. No claws or defenses. Just being.

"Good night, Sotiny," I breathed.

"Good night, Alex."

Chapter 13

Alex

Age 17

"Pssst," Tyson called out to his sister through the window. After the sucker punch she'd landed on Claurice's face, she was still grounded a month later. Not that it meant much to her anyway. She was a homebody through and through.

We peered through Sotiny's window. She was curled up, studying a textbook in the corner of her ridiculously lavished and pink room. Not by her choice of course, in fact she hated the color. Her mother however, not so much. Her room was spotless, immaculate as expected. Comparatively, Tyson's was a dump. "Boys will be boys," his mother often mused.

"Mrs. Fields snuck us some lollies," Tyson

beamed at his little sister. For him, this wasn't anything new or strange. But for her, it was a secret treat.

"Andddd..." I drawled out with a little drum roll. "She made some vanilla cupcakes." I presented a cupcake for show.

She beamed at that, closing her book and glancing in the direction of her mother's door as if she'd be busted at any time. "The ones with butter-cream icing?" she whispered, tucking a piece of the long fiery-red hair behind her ear.

Tyson nudged me, pure brother pride filling him. "I knew she'd love them."

Tyson Bryer adored his sister. In my opinion, he was the only one who showed Sotiny what family love was. I wondered if at times she kept reading those books with Harry Potter and the magical world because she somehow related to being like him, except not trapped beneath a staircase. Well, it wasn't that bad, but her mother was completely controlling of Sotiny, and yet Tyson was so obviously her pride and joy.

"Eat them quickly before Mom finds out," Tyson whispered.

"Tyson, is that you?" their mother called out. We threw the cupcake and candy into Sotiny's direction, quickly rounding the side of the house as Miss Bryer stepped out.

"You boys finished up for the afternoon already?" she asked in her thick Alabama accent.

"Nah not yet, Mom, we were thinking of going over to Billie's for a few hours to try and put together his car."

"The piece of scrap metal you were telling me about?" she asked, raising her hand to block out the sun. Her long red hair was neatly combed through. Fifty-one times exactly, every morning, Tyson had told me.

"It's coming along great," Tyson charmed her a smile.

"Well, you boys don't be too long out after dark, and how's your mother, Alex? She must be stressed with the renovations you've been having over there." She pointed next door to our house.

"Almost done now, Miss Bryer and not stressful at all." I offered her a polite smile, even though I despised the woman.

"Well make sure you're home by six. I overheard you talking to one of your friends the other night that you liked the chili con carne his mother made so I'm whipping it up for dinner tonight for you," she said, smoothing over her long blue dress.

Tyson's smile faltered. "Mom, we can't have that, Sotiny's allergic to chili, remember?"

Miss Bryer's expression didn't change in the slightest, though her smile faltered for the smallest of moments. "Don't worry there's plenty of things she can throw together for a salad. And besides at this age she needs to be educated on healthy eating, right? Us women aren't built the same as you men, we grow out quickly to the sides." She lightheartedly laughed. "Speaking of your sister, I better check on her and make sure she's studying; you know how she can get lost in those silly little books of hers." She rolled her eyes as she closed the screen door. "Don't forget to be home by six."

We both stood there, my rage boiling. I looked over at Tyson, his expression the same. The Bryer family moved in five years ago. And their mother never mentioned any father, where they came from, or how they'd acquired the mortgage on the house. Although we suspected Miss Bryer was probably related to Mrs. Dwyler who lived here and passed away five years ago. From what Tyson had told me, they never knew their father. And in Fairhope, his mother had acquired a name for herself for trying to coax married men.

"Come on, we've got to go," Tyson said reluctantly.

"Are you okay with that?" I asked.

"You know I'm not," he growled. I felt the angry ripple through my jaw. *No he wasn't.*

"Only six more months until we graduate and I'm an adult," he reminded me. The moment that happens I'm taking Sotiny away from this place."

"And where are you going to go?" I reasoned with him again. We'd gone over this so many times. "Anywhere. As long as I have my car and some savings, we'll be fine."

"You two can't live out of a car, Tyson."

"So, then I'll wait until she graduates, I'll save more money. Whenever Sotiny gives the signal we're out of here. You don't have to worry about it, it's not your problem."

My cutting glare told him otherwise.

"I appreciate your concern and I consider you my best friend. But you know as much as I do that my mother despises Sotiny and the older she gets the worse it is."

Because her daughter was a hidden beauty and the old hag was beginning to age. It was unbelievably petty.

"Don't you want to go to college or something? Maybe there's another way around it?" I suggested.

"Nah college is for Sotiny. You know she's the brains. I'll work while she goes to college."

"But she'll have to finish senior year for that, Tyson?"

"Yea so I don't have it all planned out, okay? I don't know what to do." He threw his hands up in the air. "I don't have money. I'm not smart like you and Sotiny. It's not like I'm the best player on the footy team and will get a scholarship or something. I'm just... average. I'm going to do the best I can for her since I haven't been able to do much at all now."

I furrowed my eyebrows. "I appreciate that you care for my little sister too, man." Care *was an understatement for how I felt for his sister*. "But I can deal with this. You don't have to worry, everything's going to be okay."

"She's not a broken little bird, Tyson," I gritted out. She had a voice. A big one with a decent spoonful of attitude as well. "You need to ask Sotiny what she wants. She's not still the little girl you remember."

His usual happy-go-lucky features hardened. "And what? You suddenly think you know my sister better than me?"

I gave him a cautious stare. And here was the defensive big brother act. He loved his sister, and I knew he wasn't lying when he said he'd take her away. And I selfishly hated that he'd take her from me. Nor did I have a right to feel that or even have a say in the matter. But neither did I like him keeping her out of this plan. Why didn't anyone else see her the way that I did? She wasn't some trapped little girl. If they listened only once, they'd all realize she had a lot to say.

Chapter 14

Sotiny

I hadn't spoken much to Alex. Especially after I woke up curled around his arm like a child would her favorite doll. I was certain he'd noticed, in the same way I'd noticed the feverish complexion he hosted. When I'd asked if he was sick he simply said, "You know I don't get sick." As rare as it was, he wasn't invincible either.

We hadn't yet checked into our rooms in Ithaca, already running late with our scheduled appointment with Hayden at his office, we decided it was best to have the car towed and deal with the consequences later. Fortunately, we were able to hire out a small shoebox car, much to Alex's disdain. If it wasn't for his already sniffly nose, I was certain he was going to cry about his *beloved* car.

Hayden's office was quaint. With its own sprawling property covered with methodically planted trees, it appeared to be an ornate home refurbished into office spaces. I expected something grander but was pleasantly surprised that he hadn't created an eyesore in his hometown.

"Are you sure you're feeling okay?" I asked.

"I could ask the same for you?" he said pointedly, evidently irritated by the small car that fits far less of him than his own car.

"Excuse me?"

"You know with all this new stuff? And without your regular routine?" He pivoted around his question.

"I like doing new things," I said with eyebrows furrowed. "Are you deflecting?"

"I'm fine." He stepped out of the car before my outstretched hand could measure his temperature. I swallowed, swatting away a piece of loose blonde hair that had fallen on my gray pants.

The chill of the air was a refreshing slap to the face. I hooked my coat over my arm, adjusting my beige tight-fitting sweater.

"It's not exactly what I expected," Alex confessed as he pulled out his briefcase.

"I think it's charming," I admitted. Despite being

a self-made billionaire, he was still humbled to live in his hometown.

"You said the same thing about the run-down motel we stayed in last night where we nearly froze to death."

The flashback of waking up, clinging to Alex's arm, resurfaced. I looked away, heat rising to my cheeks. *Well it'd appear my body had a mind of its own. Survival,* I argued. *To keep warm.*

A well-maintained garden and path paved the way toward the white glass door. There with hands on hips was a woman screaming into what appeared to be an office. She was no taller than me, with long brown curly hair and dark-brown eyes. She was screaming in Italian—well, reprimanding seemed more appropriate a term. Alex and I were frozen in the doorway, staring in bewilderment as a well-suited gent who also seemed preoccupied by what was happening in the office went agape at our entrance. He pushed the tip of his glasses up his nose.

"Amber," he whispered, almost too frightened to touch her shoulder and point in our direction.

The moment her blazing brown glare ensnared us, I felt like we'd been trapped by a dragon. She said nothing. A wave of pure calm washed over her.

"Hayden, your guests have arrived." She closed the door and offered us a courteous smile.

"Sorry you had to see that. I'm awfully embarrassed. I swear we're much more professional than this, I wasn't expecting you for another hour. Not that that's an excuse. I'm Amber, Hayden's assistant." She reached out her hand. A small pulse at her temple grabbed my attention. This had been the Amber we'd been negotiating with over the past few months? She carried a thick Italian accent and there was something edgy and confident to her. She packaged at around my height, all curves and tan complexion. And, by the way that we walked, in an air of authority not even I'd be daring to touch.

Alex shook her hand. "Apologies, we're here earlier than expected. The tow truck was surprisingly punctual."

"Sotiny," I said with a polite smile.

"What a pretty face to finally match the voice," she remarked. "And I still can't believe you actually got stuck at the run-down motel? I'd heard a horror story about its maintenance once."

"The horror story was probably flattering if nothing else," Alex charmed.

"And this is Gregory our accountant." Amber

moved to the side so Gregory could introduce himself and shake each of our hands.

"Sorry about that, it's always a bit chaotic here in a fun way." He glanced briefly at Amber whose glare threatened he say nothing more. I immediately liked Amber. She had that confidence and air about her that would keep any man, woman or company in check. Including Hayden Zilch by the sounds of it.

"Come, come, let me grab your coats and we'll make some coffees." She hung our coats and welcomed us inside, wriggling the handle to Hayden's office and making sure it was properly closed.

Alex and I shared a pointed glare, and a smirk twisted his expression. My eyes bulged slightly. Surely, he wasn't insinuating Hayden was in his office with someone else?

He placed his hands in his pockets, shrugging in response to my unsaid question. Were all men like this? Had I just been walking around during my twenties with no idea that people were banging left right and center with no care for protocol or professionalism in the office?

"Tea or coffee, Sotiny?" Amber repeated.

"Oh umm." I hadn't had a coffee yet but looking at the circular wall clock, it was two hours later than when I'd usually have it. "No thank you, I'll stick to water."

What might've been an old kitchen had been renovated into a kitchenette and circular table that fit eight chairs.

"I tell you what, this coffee machine is a godsend for me during winter," Amber began as she tapped out the beans to grind them.

"Wow you have an actual coffee machine in here?" Alex asked, taking a seat.

"Yea two Christmases ago Amber kept complaining about how the old cup of joe just didn't cut it. So, as you can see. Amber's machine." Gregory pointed to the elaborate looking coffee machine. "Hayden's coffee machine." He pointed to the simmering black jug of coffee.

"What beans are you using?" I asked curiously, peering over her shoulder.

"Sotiny used to be a barista through college," Alex remarked. It was one of the many jobs I had just so I could afford to stay on campus.

"Really?" Amber asked. "That's impressive. I had a friend teach me how to use one of these and I've been spoilt ever since."

"Thank you, Mr. Zilch," a woman's voice rasped from around the corner. *They* were *having sex!*

"I look forward to our ongoing business arrangements," Hayden said smoothly. "We'd be delighted to look over the sponsorship and campaign. Here let me grab your coat."

That little pulse at Amber's temple began to flare again. I sat across from Alex directing my gaze elsewhere because I was certain he wore a smug "I told you so" expression. Behind us were another two rooms and on the left a living room space and bathroom.

"Is there history in this building?" Alex asked.

"Not history per se. This was where Alex started his company when he came out of college and it's boomed ever since. He's renovated and hired staff but we're the only ones who live locally," Gregory replied.

"We've suggested a new office and expansion, maybe even a new front in a city somewhere but for the time being he's set on remaining here," Amber said, concentrating on frothing the milk.

"I don't have any reason to expand elsewhere for the time being," Hayden said, entering the room. Besides a stray lock of hair and slight redness to his cheeks he looked perfectly fine. "Everything can be done from here and what can't be we freelance out."

"How did your meeting go?" Amber asked

coolly, though it was all venom. *I liked her a lot.* The clunk of coffee was awfully deafening as she offered it to Alex who tried his hardest not to smirk.

"I think we might've reached an agreement."

"Mmm" is all she said before opening the office door behind her to grab some notes.

Inside, I noticed a whiteboard with a list of five women's names. I pointed to it curiously. "Are those some of your players?"

Amber, abashed, laughed nervously before flipping it around. "Well, that side isn't what we're meant to be looking at and you wouldn't believe me even if I told you the story behind those names."

Another stern glance between Hayden and Amber. Wow, did Hayden's PA run a tight ship. It felt like they did things a little different here. Or perhaps this was what working together for so many years looked like. That behind the professionalism they acted as a familiar unit? I'd seen it amongst some groups at *Be True* but didn't entirely understand it.

Hayden poured himself a cup of black coffee. "I'm assuming you've gone over the schedule. Simon, your columnist, has had his flight delayed but he'll be meeting us straight at the college. It's basically free for all, if you notice something you want to pitch or angle let me know. I'm just meeting with a few of the players I've scouted. Today we'll focus on the college."

It'd been a while since I'd been on any college campus and although the novelty of it seemed fun, I'd never had interest in the sports played. This was definitely going to be educational to say the least.

Chapter 15

Sotiny

I couldn't have been further out of my depth. Sports and I had never been friends. Even in college I kept my nose in my books and socializing to a minimum. I never attended any games nor did I particularly care about what our mascot was. But through the lens of Hayden and his career, it was interesting to see how he carefully selected his clients, who he thought he could best represent and those he kept a close on eye as possible future clients.

Although only a few came from Ithaca and most of his players lived in major cities and traveled the world often there was something humbling about his hometown roots. I was even somewhat envious of how he loved his hometown. I never had any intention of going back to mine. There was nothing to go back to.

I sat on the sidelines in the bleachers by the basketball courts watching a group of four college students have a "quick" game with Hayden and Alex. Simon, our columnist, suggested he'd referee. I don't know if that was from lack of sports ability or simple survival skills. *The guys were rough.*

Almost all of them had taken their shirt off by now. Even I was starting to feel effected by the heat in here—and for entirely different reasons. My eyes raked over Alex's body. I intensely studied the taught muscles, those ridiculously large arms, and the V-line that trailed beneath his waist as if I'd be examined on it within the next minute. If someone asked me to sculpt his body out of clay, I was certain I'd be pretty accurate.

Sweat beaded Alex's body, his swift movements easily able to match the young all-stars of the team. Every heavy thump had his pecks bouncing. His gaze found mine. Shamelessly, I didn't look away. This was part of what made Alex stand out and something he'd always had over me. He was able to adapt to his surroundings easily. He was magnetic and easygoing. And was capable at most things. Especially physical activities.

And I was... awkward to say the least. I also didn't want to be overshadowed by him on this project and had to utilize my own strengths, which predominately involved organization, negotiations, and contracts. But I needed to be more. I needed to be better. I'd have to be more like Alex, adaptable, especially if I wanted to live out my dream in any kind of publishing house.

Briefly, the men broke apart, congratulating one another on their game play. Simon began talking with Hayden in a flurry, showing him photos that he'd taken and suggestions of angles and side pieces.

It seemed the two worked well adapting to the sports arena, and what did I have to offer? Why was I even here?

"Hey," Alex said, passing the ball from one hand to the other. My gaze dipped to the sweat that so perfectly beaded its way down his aggressive V-line, cutting below his pants. *Get it together. You spend one night with him in your bed and now you're a feral animal.*

An animal with no experience, a self-criticizing tone crept in.

"Come throw some hoops with me."

"Absolutely not." I crossed my arms. Never in my life had I ever been good at any type of sport.

Even yoga was a stretch, and I mostly liked the "savasana" part where I laid there and did nothing.

"Come on, Sotiny, this whole week is centered around 'sporty things,'" he said, air-quoting. "You might as well join in the experience."

I chewed on my thumbnail. I didn't want to fall behind. This was for work, after all. Building business relationships and such.

"Fine," I said, standing up defiantly and jumping down the two steps. When I was close enough for only him to hear, I said quietly, "But you know my five foot four isn't going to do nada," I grumbled.

He threw his head back and laughed. "It's really only five four? I always gave you the benefit of five five. And don't worry I think your pocket rocket height will do just fine."

"Pocket rocket?" I said, mouth agape.

The four college guys turned to watch. I smoothed my blonde bob, refusing to show my embarrassment. Okay so this really wasn't in my field of expertise but nor was I going to let Alex get a leg up on me.

"Relax, I'll help you," Alex said.

"Help me magically grow one foot?" I said sarcastically, grabbing the ball from his hands.

His chuckle rolled down my spine and pooled

heat into my stomach. I hated when he made me feel that way—not in control of my own body.

I didn't dare even bounce the ball on the ground in case I didn't catch it again. *This is so not my wheelhouse.*

I sized up the hoop as if it were my next client. I was a confident and capable woman. I closed all my deals with efficiency and ease.

"Jesus, Sots, you look like you're about to tackle the pole not throw a ball into it."

"Alex," I moaned my complete psyched-up-self gone. That's when I noticed our onlookers. The four college guys sat down lazily, drinking their water and watching on with anticipation. "Why are they watching me?" I whispered feverishly. I didn't like to be seen. Especially when I wasn't particularly good at said activity.

"Because what guy wouldn't want to watch you?" My gaze snapped to his, the others nothing but a blur in the distance. "Here. I'm going to touch you so don't bite my arms off in the process."

"What do you take me for, a Chihuahua?" I snapped.

His chuckle pooled another roll of warmth into my stomach. "Never," he teased.

Alex wrapped his arms around me from behind, his hand a blazing trail until his fingers fluttered across my hand. My heart pounded and everything seemed to stop. I hated how my body reacted to him. To his touch. To his smell. To his pure masculinity and overpowering heat. His feverish heat.

"Are you burning up?" I asked.

"No." His breath was a hot flush against my ear. That single word was enough to stop me dead in my tracks. My body was an inferno, a raging combustible, fragile thing that hinged on his every word.

"Maybe I should ask one of the professional players to help me?"

"Do you really think I'm going to let any other man touch you in front of me?"

A flutter broke out in my stomach, his words weighing heavy at his possessive tone that made me feel wanted. *Needed. His.*

"Focus. You've always been good at that. This is no different. And loosen your wrists."

"I am loose," I hissed.

"Sotiny Bryer, you're as a tight as a fucking nun."

"Alex!" I said, abashed, trying to pull away from him. "I can't believe you just said that to me."

He chuckled. "Relax. I was just trying to get a reaction out of you. Come on. It's one shot."

"This is ridiculous," I said bitterly as I let him pull me back in tightly. Despite my uneasiness of knowing he was a sweaty mess... I only wanted to lean closer into him.

"Are you concentrating?" he asked, his hot breath flushing over my ear. Every part of him set my body into an uncontrollable blaze.

"Of course," I breathed. *Only breathing in the remnants of his cologne.*

"Breathe and imagine you're going to get it into the hoop. And then shoot," he said, pulling back my arms slightly. "With everything you've got, baby girl."

His hands loosened around my wrists as I focused on my target and with all the strength I could muster, I threw the ball.

The heavy thud of it hitting the backboard and skimming the ring, seemed to stop time and space. It circled the ring once before slipping outside over the edge. Almost but not quiet.

"Close!" Hayden said, clapping, breaking me from my feverish concentration. I stepped away from Alex, a vortex of cool air suddenly reminding me of everyone else in the room.

"I reckon we'll be bringing her onto the team in no time," one of the players shouted out.

When I turned to face Alex, defeated but feeling victorious all the same, I was disappointed to find him walking out of the basketball court the door closing firmly behind him.

Chapter 16

Sotiny

S imon leaned between our chairs in the rental car. "Wow this is a nice hotel, *Be True* don't skim on their getaways, do they?"

If only you saw the one we stayed at last night, I thought.

"Let's check in," Alex said quietly. He hadn't looked into my direction since the basketball game. A few more interviews, followed by a tour around the pride and joy of Ithaca College before our day was cut short in the afternoon by way of Hayden having "an urgent meeting to attend" to. I was certain that was code for booty call.

"So will we be going out for dinner or checking out some of the bars. I found this one on the Gram and it looked really nice." Simon displayed his phone, scrolling through images of food and wines.

"I'm going to have to bail tonight," Alex said, pulling out our travel bags from the boot. "But you guys go without me."

I stared at him incredulously. He wasn't his usual self. "I have a few things to attend to as well, Simon, sorry."

"Wow you guys really take this seriously, huh? I hope the workload hasn't increased for you too much, Sotiny, since Michelle's been off?" Simon asked.

"Not at all," I politely smiled. If anything, it created the opportunity for me to show my capabilities even more. I couldn't let Michelle down.

Up ahead, Alex coughed, his figure hunched ever so slightly. *Not running a fever my ass.*

The hotel consisted of two levels with a nice balcony view of the city. Flyers bombarded the reception room suggesting everything from cute cafes to waterfalls. Handing each of us our key with very little said, Alex stormed toward his room at the end.

"Okay well, see you in the morning, Alex." Simon waved him off. "Wow poor guy doesn't look too good. I've never seen him look so grumpy. Do you think we should buy him some cough medicine?"

I nudged my door open. Yes and no. Why was he so proud? He could've easily told us he wasn't feeling well. "I think he'll be fine. Enjoy your evening out, Simon."

"Sure will. And if you change your mind let me know," he said hopefully. Simon was a nice guy. He'd always been polite and tried to create small talk with me. However, this was a night I wanted to stay in.

The room was quirky, containing a queen-sized bed with thick lavender blankets. The room smelt of pine and had a forest backdrop behind the head-board. A plasma TV was erected on the wall with wooden furniture. It almost looked like a forest getaway with its own Ithaca charm. It also contained an en suite and kitchenette.

I opened the fridge out of curiosity. How nice, free milk.

Tired from the day, I began to run a hot bath. While the water ran, I scanned over the room service menu. This was going to be a perfect night in. I spread out my laptop on the dining table preparing for the next few hours of work to fill my evening with.

I slowly dipped into the hot bath, the heat

sinking into my bones immediately. Today had been interesting to say the least. This was so out of my comfort zone and yet my mind swiftly navigated the feeling of Alex holding me from behind. I dipped my face under the water, blowing bubbles. My skin felt just as scorching now as it did when I was with him.

I closed my eyes, irritated that I'd become so bothered over him and that hia damn rich cologne was all I could smell. My core throbbed, a gentle pulse beckoning me to please. I didn't want to have this reaction to him. And yet, my hand glided down my stomach of its own accord.

I couldn't give him the satisfaction, but I could use him for my own. I circled my clit, the immediate sensation running through me like lightning. How long had it been? I was so damn wound up after last night that I needed some kind of release. I knew it meant nothing to him but I found his proximity infuriating.

Biting my bottom lip and dipping a finger inside, I thought of Alex's sweaty form. The way he looked today on the basketball court. The way his arms flexed and his heavy chest pounded. I wondered what that might feel like. Lying under him, my nails digging into his side, feeling that heavy breath right before he plunged into me.

I quickened my pace, fingering myself into oblivion. There was always that little voice in my mind, reminding me that I didn't know what it actually felt like to be under him—or any man for that matter. But I'd fantasised about it so many times. My hips found a natural rhythm of their own. I imagined it felt something like this.

A low murmur escaped me. I imagined him nipping at the small lump in my throat, kissing me gently and possessively at the same time. His hot breath flushing over me as he continued to thrust. The suction of water pumped against me as I rolled my head back, eyes closing and giving way to my crazy fantasy. I could feel the swarm in my lower region building, beckoning for that long-awaited release.

"Alex," I murmured his name, fixated on those calloused hands that trailed my body. Goose bumps ran up my body from the way he'd say my name in return. The passion, need and hunger filling his gaze. He wanted me as much as I thirsted for him. Heat trailed up my legs, concentrating in one place. I slipped a second finger in, moaning at its filling pleasure.

A raspy cough in the background wavered my focus. Again, I narrowed down on the imagery of those sweaty abs and my hand brushing down every hard ridge. Another cough. Courser and more desperate this time. A small growl rippled through me as I feverishly fingered myself. Another cough.

My eyes flashed open as I slapped the water on top. *Are you serious?!* I wanted to shout at the top of my lungs. I narrowed my gaze on the surprisingly thin wall.

Not sick my ass. Tendrils of water dripped down my body as I stepped out of the bath. I'd be fucked if I was going to listen to him coughing and spluttering as I tried to enjoy a hot bath. He probably didn't even have any aspirin to bring down his fever.

I internally screamed, wanting to stomp my foot. My hot fluster had rolled over me, leaving a tense and heavy beat at my core. I searched through my handbag for aspirin and wrapped the white plush towel around me, drops splattering on the floor.

I stormed over to his room, banging on his door. On my third round of banging, he opened the door narrowing his gaze on my suspended fist. Then his gaze trailed down my body and the dripping edges of my hair. My heart sank. *He didn't look good at all.*

His face was flushed, sweat beading across his forehead. My immediate reprimand vanished as I handed him the box of aspirin. "This should help bring down the fever. If it doesn't work, text me and I'll get you something else from the store."

He stared at the aspirin, chancing another glance over my body. "Aren't you going to say I told you so?" His voice wasn't even his anymore, he sounded like he was half asleep. Those puppy dog eyes worked wonders on me. I'd never seen him look so *small*. In fact, I don't think I'd ever seen him sick.

"Of course I was right," I chided. "Now get some rest."

"Wait," Before I could leave, he grabbed my wrist. He stared down at my wrist in his, swallowed by his size. Gently, he rubbed his thumb over it, considering. "Can you stay with me for a while?"

My jaw dropped. *He couldn't be serious?* I had no secret power to make it all go away. But a jutting memory of my brother spending days with me at a time when I was sick rose up. As a child and even into my teens I'd always been frail. On some occasions, even Alex had looked after me then. I wanted to say no, to walk straight back into my hotel room and slam the door. But there was a small yearning in me, ever so slightly, that wanted to spend one more hour with him.

"Why?" My tone was cold, harsh even. *Was he*

playing me again? Was I falling for his womanizing tricks all over again?

In a small voice, he earnestly said, "Because I'm sick." Again, his gaze trailed down my body. "And you will be too if you stay out in the hallway only wearing that towel."

Simon's door squeaked open and without thought, I pushed Alex back inside and slammed the door behind me. The towel caught in the door, yanking, and I was left naked and dishevelled.

"Don't look!" I yelled, trying to cover myself up.

A smirk twitched at his lips as he shamelessly raked his gaze up my body. "As beautiful as I remember," he said before turning away and throwing the hoodie that hung over his chair toward me. "You don't ever have to hide from me, baby girl."

No, it was because of all these maddening feelings and thoughts about you that I had to cover myself up. I clutched onto his hoodie, the scent of his cologne wrapping around my senses. I checked over my shoulder to make sure he wasn't watching before quickly throwing it on. In my right mind, I should leave.

But as he slumped into his bed with a grumble to his aches, I felt lighter. Maybe he was so feverish that he wouldn't even remember any of this by the morning. *As beautiful as I remember.* I locked those words up in a small vault inside of me—something I'd wanted to hear him say for years and yet pushed away so forcefully.

"I don't know if I should stay..."

"But I'm sick." he croaked, throwing his arm over the bed and holding out his hand to me. His bottom lip quivered dramatically as I hitched my hand on my hip. "What if something happened to me tonight, wouldn't you feel guilty?"

"Rich from someone who said only hours ago he was fine. Now suddenly you're on your deathbed, huh?" He did seem pretty hopeless in this state though. Something refreshing to see instead of his usual cocky demeanor that I wanted to hit over the head half the time. I walked over to the kitchenette pouring him a glass of water for his aspirin.

"If I were on my deathbed, would you come visit me?" he asked quietly, his eyes closing and other hand hanging over his face, purposefully hiding his expression.

The sincerity in his question knocked me back. Had he asked any other time, I would've mocked him and shot him down. But this side of Alex... was different... innocent even. "Alex Fields, you've done so much dumb shit in your life, if that wasn't going to get you, then a small cold won't."

"I'm sorry," he replied as he took the glass of water from me.

"For what?"

He looked into the glass as if it held all the answers he'd been searching for. His gaze didn't reach mine as he said, "For not being there when it happened." My chest clenched and I ran cold. *No, we don't talk about that day.* "It was selfish of me and I'm sorry."

"Go to sleep, Alex."

Silence. He threw back two aspirins, downed the water, and fell back onto his stacked pillows. I dragged a chair up beside him and leant over to feel the temperature on his forehead. He was burning up bad.

"Alex, it's pretty bad."

He grabbed my hand and held it to his cheek. "I just pushed it too far during the game is all."

I felt stiff under his touch and spell. So many times, I'd wanted to sink into a moment like this with him. But there was too much history. Too much anger and hurt. And yet, I wanted to give myself at least one moment to enjoy what might've been. To live out that fantasy at least once if we'd actually lived out our days as husband and wife. I sat down in the chair, my arm outstretched as he clutched to it like his last breath.

"I miss him," he said honestly. My heart squeezed. I gently traced my thumb over his cheek-bone trying to usher him to sleep but distract myself at the same time.

"I miss him too," I admitted.

Chapter 17

Alex
Age 17

At the sound of smashing plates against tiling, I pushed through the screen door, unsure of exactly what I'd see.

"How could he not leave his wife for me?" Miss Bryer's voice howled through the kitchen. "You! It's because you weren't polite enough when he visited. Do you really think just because you're pretty you can do whatever you want, including ruining my life?"

Another crash against the wall.

I bounded through their living room and into the kitchen. Rage flashed through me as the scene unfolded once I rounded the corner. Sotiny was huddled behind the island bench, covering her face as shards of porcelain rained around her.

"Alex?" Miss Bryer shrilled, surprised. She scanned the kitchen as if looking for an explanation. "What are you... what are you doing here? Umm Tyson isn't here? We were just—"

"You're coming with me," I said to Sotiny, ignoring Miss Bryer. With rage burning through me like fire, I'd burn the whole house with her mother in it just to get Sotiny out of this situation.

Without delay, Sotiny reached her hand out to me, that pale skin a beam of light in the narrowing darkness of my tunnel vision. Her mother's words came in waves and fits, I couldn't comprehend. I couldn't think or hear clearly. I picked Sotiny up and cradled her close to my chest, leaving the kitchen.

A small shake ran through Sotiny, and I pinned her closer to my chest. Despite her obvious fear, not one single tear escaped. I'd never seen her cry. Even amongst this abusive hell hole. All that oppressive terror and vile words stunting any emotion to leak through. She was conditioned like an inconvenient discarded doll.

"Alex! We were just talking. This is normal family stuff," her mother tried to argue, following me out the front screen door.

I was getting her the fuck out of here.

"Hey, man!" Tyson said as he pulled up short in

their driveway. His face paled. "Sots? What happened?"

"Tyson!" Miss Bryer shouted from behind. Rage bubbled over and I nudged past Tyson. *Why wasn't he here?*

"Hey!" Tyson grabbed my shoulder and yanked me back. "What happened?"

My grip was iron tight on Sotiny.

"It's a misunderstanding," Miss Bryer reasoned. "Sotiny and I were having a little discussion."

"She was throwing fucking plates at her, Tyson!"

Tyson paled, his gaze turning on his mother.

"Where the fuck were you?" I demanded. Sotiny flinched at my harshness.

Tyson's gaze flicked back to me. "What?" he snapped.

"If you're so great at protecting your fucking sister, then where were you?"

"Alex!" I could hear my mother's voice in the background.

"Put my sister down!" Tyson's temper snapped as he tried to yank me back.

"Stop!" Sotiny cried out. "Alex put me down."

My heart pounded through my chest. I wanted to hurt anything and everything. I'd burn down the whole fucking world for her so she wouldn't have to deal with this shit anymore. She stepped away and that's when I noticed the red on her white shirt, blood. A gash, thick enough to need stitches. All I saw was red.

"Where the fuck were you?" I shoved Tyson, any kind of rationality fleeing. I hated him. I hated myself. Why weren't we eighteen yet? Why hadn't we done anything? *Why hadn't I done anything?*

A sudden rage filtered Tyson's expression, coming to a rational conclusion. "Dude, are you in love with my sister?" he demanded, shoving me back.

I swung, connecting, red rising from Tyson's lip. He charged me, lifting me off the ground and throwing me into the ground. We rolled around. Hit for hit. Ribcages pounded. *She wasn't some fragile little doll. She deserved better than this.*

"Alex!" I heard my mother shout again. Strong muscle-bound hands grabbed at me and Tyson. My dad grabbed me from behind as my older brother yanked Tyson back.

"Get off me!" I screamed.

"Son, you need to get a hold of yourself!" Dad yelled.

"Alex! This isn't the way!" my mother repri-manded me. A cold chill and disappointment laced her tone.

"Tyson are you okay?" Miss Bryer cooed running to his side. Tyson shrugged my brother off and swiped blood from his lip. He pulled away from his mother and stormed toward me.

"I warned you!" Tyson pointed at me, death in his eyes. "Stay away from my sister."

"Get off our lawn!" Miss Bryer screamed.

"We're so sorry for any issues our sons caused," my mother apologized.

"Leave it for now," my brother ensued as he grabbed me by the neck and tugged me toward our house. A few of the neighbors had stepped out of their homes, watching the commotion. I swiped my own lip, seeing red. My light-blue shirt was stained red from Sotiny's shoulder.

She stared at me doe-eyed, those piercing blue eyes a fragment of the chaotic ocean I knew lay beneath. *Why? Why did she let her mother treat her like that? Why did she think that was all she was worth and deserved?*

"Not now, son," Dad repeated as he tugged me toward our house. *Not now meant to turn a blind eye... again.*

A deep-rooted hatred filled Tyson's stare as he watched us walk away. In a matter of minutes, I'd lost my best friend but a heavier weight replaced it as Sotiny stared at me with such disdain.

"Come on, we need to take you to the hospital," Tyson pulled at his little sister, and ever so slowly, she looked away, our locked gaze broken.

Chapter 18

Alex

The past had been catching up to me more than I'd like. I knew it'd be hard living in the same city as her. I knew it'd near strangle the air out of me working so closely with her. And yet, every day my gaze naturally gravitated toward her like she was my very next breath. Memories of that night, our wedding, the vows taken and the chaos that ensued, it was on some repetitive, torturous loop. I had no right to her, and yet she was all I wanted. Even after all these fucking years.

Since the night I'd gotten sick, Sotiny and I danced around each other professionally. That wall between us was erect once again. My fever broke and Sotiny was nowhere to be seen that morning. I vaguely remembered our conversations and was particularly fond of the memory of her shrill voice and trying to cover herself up when the towel had been eaten by the door.

My cock throbbed, a twitch at my lips transforming into an arrogant smile.

"What are you smiling at?" Sotiny demanded, as if self-conscious and all knowing. She'd barely spoken to me all day.

"Just a pleasant memory," I said, sliding my gaze over to her. I thought Damon and Michelle were rotten for putting us on this project together. Granted I would've stirred the pot and done the same to either one of them if they were in my position. But despite its highs and lows so far, I'd actually enjoyed spending time with her like this on the project. There was a sliver of normality, whatever that looked like for us.

"We've got some great shots here," Simon said, coming to a stop between us. We were at the local football stadium where a big barbecue cookout was being served. Their local all-star footballer James Parker had returned to his hometown for a charity fundraiser.

Hayden and Amber were a flurry around the media, orchestrating James's time and image. Simon was the first privileged to interview him with exclusive shots. We'd taken group photos with the intention to print an online exclusive interview gauging interest the new readership might have.

Sotiny pulled the buzzing cell out of her pocket. "It's Michelle, I'll be back."

I was certain half of the town had arrived to celebrate their local hero. Hayden and James were strolling over, heads dipped low and hands in pocket as they spoke. Running over the figures and forecast, I knew the sports edition would be a hit, especially considering the clients I'd approached for ad space and sponsorship. I promised Damon he wouldn't have to stress about a thing, and I hoped that held true.

"This is an exciting opportunity for you as well, no?" James asked Hayden. The tanned football player was built like a brickhouse. On top of that, he had that quality star gleam about him, his pretty face was an added bonus. At only twenty-four, he had a lot riding for him. "Being the face of a big shot magazine. Come on, Hayden, you've come leaps and bounds!" he said enthusiastically. The two seemed more like friends than business acquaintances, but I realized, much like my own charm, Hayden had that quality about him.

"Will you be coming out for dinner with us?" Hayden asked James.

"Sorry, man, I have to go back to Chicago tonight, considering the amount of press releases you've scheduled for me."

Hayden shrugged. "I'm sure your bank account's disappointed."

James grinned, a boyish wide-spread smile crossing his features.

"By the way, have you spoken with Marley recently?" Hayden asked carefully.

James's wide grin slowly dropped. "You know I haven't spoken to her since we broke up."

"It's been what five years now?"

"Six," he said flatly. "Anyways, that's behind me. I'm going to quickly speak to Adam. I'll catch you on the way out." He tapped Hayden on the shoulder and jogged off.

Hayden shook his head. "The kid's matured but still has a fair way to go."

"Why's that?" I asked curiously.

"Because I'm pretty sure Marley's almost six-year-old son is a spitting image of him when he was a kid."

"Oh shit. One-night fling?"

"High school sweethearts."

"Oh, wow. What are you going to do about it?"

"Nothing for the time being. That's his journey. If he's not ready to meet with her then it's on him but I don't think he has any idea. And as it stands, he's plastered as one of the most-eligible bachelors in the country, I hope to work off that for a little longer."

"Family man doesn't sell as much, ey?"

"It does, but I can stick to what I know here," he laughed to himself. "What about you? Would you consider yourself a family man?"

I considered it momentarily. I was selfish as all hell. But I did care for my family. I didn't visit them nearly enough but with my older brother living in Seattle and my parents back at Fairhope. I hadn't found a reason to go back. Not since Sotiny left there anyway. "I'm probably not suited to it either," I admitted.

"I think I'm going to try and settle down," Hayden admitted.

I almost choked on my next mouthful of water. He laughed patting me on the back theatrically.

"Is it that unbelievable?"

"I just didn't pick you as the settling type. You have your eye on someone particular?"

"Five actually?"

I narrowed my gaze. Five, damn that was impressive, even I'd only reached as high as a foursome. "Five? Is that really the definition of *settling down?*"

"No as in five candidates. Five women who over the years I've had long term sex with. You probably saw the whiteboard with the list of women. Amber told me not to tell anyone but..." He shrugged. "It starts to feel a bit empty at some point. Casual sex I mean. And I only know what I know and that's fucking women for both our pleasure. The emotional stuff is a little more difficult for me, so I'll be going celibate until I figure out whose personality I'm better suited to."

Now I laughed.

He chuckled. "Amber reacted the same way."

"You go alright, Hayden Zilch," I said. At first, I was weary of him, but especially in the last week I realized he might not be all that bad. I supposed we were more similar than I'd like to admit.

Chapter 19

Sotiny

I was buzzing with excitement when I ended the call with Michelle. Not only was she impressed by what we'd covered in Ithaca and how swimmingly the transition for the new sports edition was coming along, but she also had personal news for me. Apparently, a good college friend of hers and editor in chief of a publishing house had an opening for an editorial role and suggested I put my name forward. My heart pounded with anticipation.

"Are you okay?" Alex asked, sitting beside me as we ate dinner at the local ale house with Amber and Hayden. Simon had since returned to Manhattan and Gregory had already made plans with his wife and children. I took a mouthful of the bitter ale, swigging it down in good favor. I really hated the stuff.

I took another mouthful of my Caesar salad, my mind preoccupied with the potential of this being something great.

"I still can't believe you told them about the list," Amber chastised Hayden. She rolled her eyes, bemused. "I outright laughed at him when he came up with it."

Ah and there was that. I didn't know whether to be disgusted or impressed by Hayden's ambitions in creating a list of five women in hopes of trying to settle down. Was it really that difficult for a former playboy to settle down? I eyed Alex from the side. Would it be near impossible for him as well? How difficult was it to be faithful? Not that I had much experience to go off, considering I'd never been in any type of romantic relationship. Unless my intimate toys counted as a relationship.

"I laughed at him when he told me as well," Alex admitted. "And thank you for the offer for those tickets and game in Chicago, I'll let you know if I can make it or not."

"No problem and bring whoever you'd like. Then we can throw back a couple of these as well," Hayden motioned to the waitress, indicating another round for him and Alex.

Amber took a sip of her red wine and cut into her

steak. As the two men discussed sports, Amber drew her attention to me. "How long have you been working for *Be True* now?"

"A little over twelve months, I've really enjoyed it. My focus was mostly on literature prior but I've learnt a lot since. The Brogardt family are wonderful to work for."

"I've only read and heard good things about them. After we were approached I did some research on the company and family. The only thing I could pull up was some unfaithful scandal around Damon Brogardt—"

"Amber," Hayden reprimanded.

"I wasn't finished." She eye rolled him. "But I'm glad to hear he found someone like Clover. I haven't met her personally yet, but I've heard so many stories about her through Hayden. I guess all good things come to those who wait. Anyway, enough of that before I get into more trouble," she jested. "Do you plan on staying with the Brogardt family for a while?"

An uncomfortable tension ran through me. "Well yes and no."

I felt Alex's gaze land on me.

"I do have intention eventually to shift over into a publishing house. I've loved the opportunity that's been given to me at *Be True* and how it runs but my passion has always laid in literature, more specifically young adult. I'd like to eventually be able to step into a role that aligns with my true passion."

"That's news to me?" Alex quietly added.

My throat felt tight. Why did I feel so apprehensive to continue any part in this conversation with Alex listening in? I found myself locking away the news Michelle had informed me about today.

"That sounds like a great plan to me," Amber congratulated. "Well, I hope that you receive what it is you're chasing. You deserve every bit of it." She raised her red wine.

"Cheers to finding what we're looking for," Hayden merrily said. Our glasses clinked and we all took a sip. Alex threw back the rest of his and seemed overly grateful for the waitress who brought the next. I couldn't help but notice a cold resolve about him and I'd remained quiet for the rest of the meal.

The evening was pleasant, merry even after the pints started kicking in. I didn't mind Ithaca and its small-town charm.

The drive home was quiet, a heavy tension rested between Alex and me. Despite how well we'd been interacting lately, the mood seemed dampened.

I thought he'd be a little more excited considering he had his Mustang back.

He continued gripping the steering wheel, studiously looking through the streets.

"What's wrong, Alex?" I asked, suffering under the tension.

"It's nothing," he said, licking his lips. "It's just you never mentioned anything about wanting to go into literature and publishing before."

"It's all I ever spoke about when I was a teen."

"Yea but, you know what I mean. Since you moved to New York. I thought you were happy at *Be True*?"

"And I am but—"

Alex slammed on the brakes, his hand stretching out in front of me and pinning me to the seat. The small dog that ran out onto the road in front of us froze and quivered right in front of us. We both slammed back into the seat, my heart caught in my throat. The moment we screeched to a stop, the small canine bolted into the distance.

Panic washed over me. Painful memories rising to the surface so abruptly it was suffocating.

"You're okay," Alex said in what sounded like from a distance. My breathing became erratic and labored.

"I need out!" I yelled. "I just need—" I fumbled with the stupid seat belt. In a swift movement, Alex unclicked it. I barged open the door, relieved by the fresh air that hit my face. Alex was by my side in an instant.

"Hey, look at me." He cupped my face. "You're okay, okay?"

I shook feverishly. But I wasn't. This wasn't okay. The memories that came instantly to the surface near paralyzed me. *It had never been okay.*

"Hey." His voice was a soothing coo, a beacon to come back to. I gripped onto his voice, watching his lips as he spoke. "You're okay. *We're both okay.*"

I nodded, trying to keep my breathing at a steady pace. He pulled me in, trapping my arms to his chest. His warmth and smell encompassed me. The rise and fall of his chest a soothing reminder to steady my own.

I breathed him in, closing my eyes and embracing the tranquillity in just being. Here. Now. Safe. *We're okay.* I pushed those looming thoughts and memories away, the terror of being sixteen and not quite yet understanding how my world was about to change.

"Sots, are you okay?" Alex quietly asked after

what felt like a lifetime of being in his embrace, but a blip in time that I wanted to last forever more.

I looked up into his concerned, shadowed green eyes. If only he'd been there on that day to tell me "it's going to be okay." Not that it ever was. But being in his embrace now, I realized all I wanted then was comfort. All I *needed* was someone to tell me it wasn't my fault.

His breath lightly danced on my face, a warm reminder that I was alive and here.

"Thank you, Alex," I said quietly, still staring at those beautiful lips. Another memory surfacing, the reminder of how they felt and how he tasted. For all the hurt that those lips had inflicted... there always remained that small spark of need and desire. Countless times, I was curious about them again, trying my hardest to push him away. And yet... here he was. Like he had been the last year. Always within reaching distance and it was me who made sure he stayed at arm's length.

The temptation was there to kiss him, only a breath away. And in the way his heavy gaze stared back at me, I was certain he was feeling the same. Like an intoxicating spell swirling between us, seeing who might give in to it first.

It felt like he'd hang off every word I'd say. But I

had to push him away gently. Steadily, I said with tension rolling through me, "I think… we should get going again."

He looked defeated, his shoulders sagging ever so slightly. His power and force around me too hard not to be tempted by. I felt like I'd been in a haze. My heart thrummed for other reasons now. Alex Fields was a temptation that was slowly erasing any logic. From all the hurt and pain he'd caused in the past— my body only demanded one thing. The one thing I'd sworn I'd never give him and that was my heart and body again.

Chapter 20

Alex

The moment I slammed the brakes on the car, I knew it'd send her back in time and flare those ugly tucked-away memories. And yet, all I could think about was how I could steal that suffering away from her. Take away all the pain and fright. And then all I could think about was kissing her. Selfishly burning with the need to caress her and make it better in the only way I knew how. But she didn't need my comfort nor did she want it. She made that abundantly clear.

Despite all of that, I just couldn't drop the idea of her moving elsewhere. She'd given me no real answer or insight as to what brought up this sudden change or desire to move on. Or maybe it'd been something she wanted all along and I'd been too ignorant to realize it. "But I thought you were enjoying working at *Be True*?"

She sighed, seemingly not surprised that I was bringing it up again. "I am, it's an incredible opportunity. But you know my heart's always laid in literature."

"And Michelle knows about this?"

"She's aware. I'm grateful for her, even though she knew that I might not stay long term she still saw something in me and offered me the opportunity to work with her. So if or when something comes up with a publisher I'm going to consider it."

"In New York?" My heart tightened as the question escaped me. I'd become so accustomed to having her around that I hadn't considered she might leave again. Leave *me* again.

"Wherever will have me."

"What about those books you were writing?"

She laughed. "Nobody will read those."

"I would."

Her head snapped to me quickly, surprised by my quick response. *I'd live off the air you fucking gave me, if you'd permit it.* I paused in the hallway, my eyebrows knitting together, confused by the sudden realization.

Casually walking ahead to our hotel room, she

quietly added, "You know, I always wondered if it was sheer coincidence that I ended up working for the exact same firm as you or with how close you are to the Brogardt family if you did something behind the scenes."

Clever girl, as always. "You should be more confident in your portfolio, Miss Granger."

She seemed to think into the distance about that. We were walking closely together, my attention drawn to her featherlight hand dancing closely to mine, her perfume that smelt of Jasmine crawling up my nose. All of her so pocket-sized and reachable.

She stopped outside her door, sifting through her handbag for the keys.

"I know that you don't necessarily enjoy your time with me," I admitted. "But I've really enjoyed this week." I knew we had our differences and history, but I was so sick of going around in circles.

She seemed conflicted. I could never read her mind when she harbored that stony expression. "I don't hate you." It was a soft whisper but admission enough.

And yet I'd heard her say it so many times. Felt her wrath when she stared at me so distantly and hatefully.

Carefully, she added, "But that doesn't mean I

don't want you to sign the divorce papers either, especially for when I move on again. I don't know, maybe we were brought to the same place to finalize that chapter and open a new door."

Move on. This woman drove me fucking mad. I fought every urge in my body to grab her and claim her as mine. *She was mine. Paper or no paper in wedlock.*

"Don't look at me like that," she said quietly.

"Like what?" I growled.

"Like I'm your next one-night stand and you're going to devour me whole." Her gaze was penetrating.

She was never meant to be a one-night stand. Flashbacks of her drunken words on our wedding night crept in. She thought I was nothing but a playboy. And that had been true. But it never applied for her.

"The one-night stand rule would never apply for you, I've told you that already." My voice was foreign, distantly possessive and primal. My cock throbbed at the mere thought of being with her. If she would have me.

She licked her bottom lip, a hitched breath. Silence.

"I might've made a lot of mistakes in my life, but this won't be one of them."

"What won't—"

I grabbed her chin possessively, looking down on her. I gave her only a fleeting moment. A split decision, if she'd choose to run or not. She hissed under the sudden pull, her eyes hungry and pleading. "Alex." Her whisper was a command. I refused to give her the option to run anymore.

My lips were on top of hers, my size pushing her against the door, barricading anyone else from seeing the beauty and vulnerability that rolled through her. One of her hands curled through my hair, the other fluttering about with the door.

Her quick and clumsy tongue elicited curse words as she struggled to open the door. I chuckled stroking down her arm and clicking the key over. The moment it creaked open, I picked her up and hitched her legs around my waist.

Her hands rolled through my hair. A small gentle moan escaped her, sending a jolt straight through to my cock.

"Alex," she moaned through kisses, her tongue a quick fire against mine. *These lips, the ones I'd agonized over years...*

"It's okay I'm not going to do anything to you tonight."

She grabbed a chunk of my hair and pulled it back, breaking our kiss. Her gaze was a steely blue.

"What do you mean by that?"

I contemplated her. My rock-hard cock pounding for only one thing. But I was almost certain... she wouldn't be ready. Not yet.

"Tell me you're still a virgin?"

That stare was enough to cut a man to his knees and leave him to bleed out for days.

"Let me please you tonight, baby girl." I cupped her face.

"I want you to fuck me," she demanded.

I chuckled pressing a kiss to her throat. A small yelp escaped her when I bit down, marking the same spot. "I will soon," I promised.

I laid her out on the bed, unbuttoning her jeans and tugging them off. She laughed as she was being pulled away and off the bed with them. "Alex, my legs are attached."

The pink lacy underwear was a gentle surprise. I dipped down to my knees at the side of her bed, admiring what lay beneath. This perfect pussy that had driven me mad for so many years.

"Alex, I want to watch you as well," she said

shyly, propping herself up onto her elbows. Amongst the dimly lit room, her gaze lit up like a wild storm. She propped up further to remove my jacket, slowly. Her shaky hands peeled off my shirt. She reached for my belt and I caught her hand. "I want to see you."

"No sex tonight," I breathed. *What kind of monster was I turning into? When had I ever said no to sex?*

"Why?" she growled. "Is it because you think I don't know what I'm doing?"

I chuckled. "Baby girl, I think you know exactly what you're doing. When I fuck you for the first time, I want you to be ready for me. I want to pound that tight pussy until you're bruised and mark every inch. But you'll need to be ready."

"I'm ready," she whispered, heat streaking across her cheeks.

"Really?" I growled, standing back up, then lying on top of her. Her hands clutched to my ribs, those gentle little claws of hers sinking in. I rubbed my unbuttoned jeans against her heat, a small moan escaping her.

"Tell me how many fingers you use on yourself."

Her eyes blazed with fire. I rubbed against her again, her eyes going half-mast at the stimulation.

My little tightly wound bunny so sensitive to the slightest of touches.

"Two," she breathed out.

"Good girl." I pinched her clit through the pink panties, another little moan escaping her. *Fuck. Had she let anyone else touch her like this?*

I circled, the grip of her hands tightening on my ribs as her eyes rolled back into her head. I slipped my hand into her panties, the slickness of her pussy forcing my cock to become painfully hard against my jeans. I rubbed her entrance, watching every flicker of uncertainty and pleasure roll through her.

I dipped my finger in, her thighs immediately clenching over my hand. A small moan escaped her as I thrusted slowly in and out, creating a rhythm. After every pump, a desperate plea escaped from her mouth. My cock pressed painfully hard against my jeans. I lifted her shirt, the matching pink bra sending me into a wild stupor. How I wanted to come all over those tits and stomach.

I slipped a second finger in, that tiny moan breaking me. I bent over, grabbing her lips and rolling my tongue against hers. Her hips rolled, fucking my palm as I slammed into her. I slipped my other hand under her bra, those hand-sized tits I'd been thinking about for so long exactly the fill I thought they'd be. I pinched her nipples and her eyes burst open with an unexpected gasp.

"Too much?" I cautiously asked, all hot breath and panting. She seemed unsure at first, then slowly shook her head. I pinched again, rolling it between my thumb and finger, another hiss escaped, her eyes wide.

"Fuck, Sots," I said, looking over her again. This perfectly built little body. I wanted more. *Needed* more. My cock throbbed a ridiculous beat and need coursed through me.

"I want to touch you," she argued. "Alex, get your cock out."

I chuckled. "You have such a filthy mouth," I encouraged, dipping down to kiss her again.

"That's ironic coming from the guy who told me I was tighter than a nun the other day."

I threw back my head and laughed. But as I thrust my fingers into her again, could she dare say I was wrong.

"Stop," she breathed. I pulled out. She leapt off the bed, her lips crashing to mine, clumsily and passionately. She dropped to her knees on the side of the bed, her hands rolling around for my jeans. She pulled them down and her eyes went wide with bewilderment, a small lump forming in her throat as she pulled down my underwear.

She gulped as my cock sprung free. "We're going to take baby steps, little virgin," I purred. "But I've imagined for the longest time you bouncing on my cock. You'll fit, baby girl. But tonight's about you."

A small defiant humph came out of her as she tucked her sharp blonde bob behind her ears and knelt over. My cock growing impossibly harder at attention. Her delicate tongue trailed from the base to the tip. She grabbed either side of my thighs, nails digging in as she bent over and took me in her mouth.

"Fuck," I growled as those perfect lips of hers scraped against my cock. She became daring, getting a feel for me as she began to dive deeper, taking me into the back of her throat. I threaded my fingers through her hair as she bobbed. I leaned back, a guttural growl escaping.

My cock twitched and slowly she pulled away, a little popping noise sounding through the room. She placed one delicate finger on her tongue and extracted a dollop of precum. Assessing it, she purposefully narrowed her gaze on me as she licked it, sucking on her finger. *Fuck.*

"I want you bent over that mattress right now,

Sotiny Bryer so I can spank that sweet little ass of yours and eat you out."

"I want you," she said, her face laced with pure need.

"I've got you, baby girl," I said, lifting her back onto the bed and pushing aside her panties. I dove my tongue into her sweet pussy, lapping up the taste of her. I stroked myself, the constant need to dive into her excruciating.

Her legs folded over my shoulders as I ate her out like she was my last fucking meal. I sucked on her clit, the little bud of nerves forcing a twitch in her leg. I stretched her out. Three fingers this time, fucking her like a madman, visualizing my cock inside of her instead.

"Please," Sotiny begged through heavy breaths. "Alex, I need you inside of me."

"Not yet," I mumbled around her clit.

"But I'm going..."

"I know." I sucked harder, pounding her sweet pussy. Her legs tightened around my shoulders pulling me in deeper. She arched into the bed, her body bucking as she came with a loud scream.

Pulses constricted my finger as I kept at a steady rhythm. She sloshed, oozing around my fingers as I continued to suckle and flick my tongue over her bud.

"Fuck, Alex!" she screamed again as another wave came over her. My tightly wound up little doll was falling apart in front of me. I clamped down on my cock, not wanting this to be over for the both of us. I wasn't ready but fuck I wanted to come inside of her.

I pushed apart her legs further, lapping up every part of her. The taste and smell of her was my complete undoing.

"Alex, I want you to come on me," she begged.

"What about your pretty little bra?" I hedged as I grabbed my cock again.

"Fucking stand up!" she demanded.

Another pulse shot down my cock. She sat upright, her knees bent beneath her. "Stand up," she demanded again. I rose, her head leveling at my chest, that sharp gaze following me the entire time. She wrapped her hand around my cock, palming it with efficiency.

Virgin or not, fuck me, she knew what she was doing.

"Are you going to come for me baby?" Sotiny asked, shamelessly staring at my cock as she palmed it.

I rolled my finger over her bottom lip. "That filthy mouth of yours is going to get you in trouble," I gritted out.

"I hope so. Now come for me," she commanded.

Fuck. This beautiful, wicked creature whose pleasure was for only me to see.

"I'm almost there," I admitted. *Fuck. I'd come undone so quickly.*

"I want you to make a mess of me, Alex. Like you'd always promised," she breathed.

That sent me over the edge. I pushed into her hand, my cum spilling over her stomach and chest. I growled. Every pulse a relief.

She pushed up, reaching for my face and pulling me in for a hungry, needy kiss. She wriggled beneath me, her hand still gliding over my cock until I had nothing else to give. She pressed her forehead to mine, our heavy breathing slowing to an even rhythm.

"You ruined my bra," she joked.

"Then I suppose I'll have to buy you a new one."

I kissed her gently and with an unspoken promise that I would try better this time. I could be better, if only she'd let me in.

"You're not going to run away by tomorrow morning, are you?" I asked quietly.

"Firstly, this is my room. And secondly, no not until you at least deliver on your promise and fuck me."

She rolled onto her back, all beaten and exhausted. Damn, everything about her was perfect. Especially that sharp and wicked tongue of hers.

"Come and lay beside me, Alex." She patted the bed. I wanted to clean her up immediately but in an exhausted heap followed her instructions. With jeans still around my ankles, I rolled onto my back beside her.

We stared up at the ceiling, a silence rolling over us and then thoughtfully, she added, "I think I have carpet burn on my knees."

I laughed, rolling her on top of me so she could rest her head on my chest. "Baby girl, that's going to be the least of your worries soon."

After another long silence, she asked, "Did you choose not to have sex with me because you'd have to throw me to the side after you did?"

"No." I angled myself around to look into her eyes. "I'd never throw you to the side. I just didn't want your first time being in a hotel room. You deserve something more special."

"Alex, I'm a woman in her thirties. I think by now I don't need 'special,' I need it to be done."

If that were the truth, she would've had it done, years ago. Any man would be so lucky to have her.

"Why haven't you given yourself to anyone?" I asked carefully.

She was silent for a moment, folding back into my chest to cover her face. Quietly, she admitted, "Nobody ever felt right. None of them were you."

Chapter 21

Sotiny

I'd woken up in Alex's arms. The past year's tension culminating to the point of no return and now seems to have eased... slightly. It terrified me that I felt so comfortable in his arms. How right it had felt and how tempting it was to stay hidden away in this hotel room forever. But as fate would have it, we had a very special event planned for the day.

Yawning, I rhetorically asked, "Remind me how we ended up at Clover's mom's house again." We were parked outside Clover's mother's house, peering up at the charming two-story home.

Alex chuckled. "Oh, come on, my mother would've done the same thing," he said, rubbing his thumb over my hand as we sat in the car parked on the street. Whatever this thing was between us, for now, I chose to embrace it, if only for the weekend. I didn't want to clam up on him the following morning like I'd always done. Because in truth last night was one of the most memorable nights of my life and I was on the verge of begging for more. "If anything, it's a reminder I'm way overdue visiting the parents sometime soon."

"When was the last time you visited them?" I asked, trying to distract myself from the arousing thoughts flickering through my mind.

"Last Christmas. You?"

Silence filled the car. "I don't know, about ten years ago. I don't even know if she still lives in that same house."

Quietly, he added, "She does."

The heaviness was an old wound and burden I'd pushed away so long ago. "Well, I hope Clover's mother likes champagne," I dully cheered, holding up the bagged bottle Alex and I'd bought her.

With what looked to be an identical version of Alex's car, but a deep-red, Hayden pulled up behind us. I retracted my hand out of Alex's, noticing his immediate frown.

"I don't want anyone knowing or asking about 'this.'" I pointed between Alex and me.

"*This?*" he queried.

"You know, whatever the sex stuff is between us." He chuckled. "Alex!" I exclaimed. "I'm serious."

"Okay, okay, okay. If that's how you want to play it, then fine."

"Play it?"

"Relax, Sotiny, I'm just pulling your tail." I stared at him, lips pursed as Hayden glanced over Alex's car, impressed. I never quite understood men and their fascination with cars.

"Looks like I made good timing then," Hayden said, showing off a birthday bag with an attached balloon.

"I don't think many others have shown up yet," I said looking down the empty street.

Alex pointed to Damon's car. "I think Clover and Damon are here."

Hayden chuckled. "You two didn't get the memo, huh? You know we're here to help set up right? It's basically the right of passage in the Clover's household. Sorry if you actually thought this was a day off." He winked.

In a weird way, Hayden had started feeling like more of a friend than a business agreement.

"Who's that?" Alex asked, pointing in the direction of the blonde-haired woman, arms crossed over her chest.

Hayden blew out a breath. "That is Megan. Clover's younger sister. And it goes without saying, she's completely off-limits."

"I didn't pick Clover to be the overprotective type?" Alex said.

"Hmmm." Hayden licked his lips. "That rule seemed to have applied only to me when Clover and I became good friends in college."

"My brother used to be like that, wouldn't let any of his friends near me either," I said, mixed emotions running through me.

"You don't say?" Hayden said pointedly to Alex who was shadowing me as we stepped out of the car.

We walked past sad rosebushes, trimmed down from the cold season.

"Hayden Zilch, is that you?" Megan asked, still with arms crossed. "You haven't changed a bit."

She was even more beautiful up close. Both the sisters were in their own way because they looked nothing alike, the only resemblance being their nose. She held out her arms in a welcoming hug.

At first, Hayden seemed hesitant, which unusual considering how friendly he was to every woman I'd seen him with. I wondered if Clover's threats were ringing through. "You've changed a fair bit, but I suppose I'm remembering you as a seventeen-year-old. Wow, the little sister of Clover Granture is all grown up now."

Alex and I shared a look. It felt nostalgic almost to watch. It felt like *us*.

"Hey! We spoke about my sister being off-limits," Clover jokingly said, pulling Megan back through the front door. Damon shadowed her, the light shadow normally on his face has slowly thickened into the outline of a beard. It was always so different seeing them outside of work in a social gathering. I never quite knew how to interact with them, like it wasn't my place to be here.

"Pfft, you couldn't handle me, sweet, sweet, Hayden," Megan teased, slapping him on the chest. "Ooh, and look, he's just as toned as back when he played footy. Good for you."

"What are you all going on about now?" an older woman's voice sang out. "Stop blocking the doorway and let our guests in before they freeze to death."

The woman who I assumed to be Clover's mother had a contagious kind of smile and warmth to her green eyes. She offered the same persona as Alex's mother and reminded me of the few times I spent with her in their home.

"Ahh, Hayden. I haven't seen you in years, but I've heard all good things that you've been keeping yourself busy with. Built yourself a nice retirement I hear," she said with a welcoming smile.

"Mom!" Megan chastised.

"I try my hardest," Hayden said with fake modesty. "And this is for you. Happy Birthday! Not looking a day over twenty-one."

She laughed wickedly. "Still the charmer I see." Her gaze drifted over to us. "Wow they breed them differently in New York don't they? I don't think I've had so many young men in my home for years."

"If ever," Megan added.

Her mother waved her off. "And what a beautiful little gem," she said, giving me a hug. I froze under the friendliness. "You must be Sotiny and Alex. Damon and Clover have told me so much about you two. Welcome. Welcome." Before I could completely shake off my stupor, she moved over and gave Alex a welcoming hug.

"Oh, this is for you." I offered her the present.

"Ooh I do like some champagne. Thank you."

"It gives her the giggles," Megan added. "Ethan! Christian! Come and introduce yourself to our guests."

Two young boys, no older than ten, hurtled

down the stairs, both politely murmuring their hellos under their breath.

They seemed almost remote from the stocky men who stood in the living room. I didn't entirely blame them for it.

"Give them a couple minutes they'll be out of their shell in no time."

"Your kids?" Alex asked. I was certain I could've felt some unresolved tension between Hayden and Megan but if their father was in the picture maybe she was the one that got away. Or maybe I'd read too many damn romances.

"Yea. This is the little tribe here," she said adoringly, cupping both their heads to her waist. "Now we're about to help Grandma clean up the backyard okay."

"Coffee, drinks, snacks are all through here in the kitchen." Mrs. Granture walked us through the living room where photos were plastered across the wall. There was a gentleman in some who I assumed was Clover's and Megan's father who'd passed, and amongst all the photos of the kids, I noticed there was no father in any picture. "Grab what you want but, we have four hours to turn this place into a party no one's going to forget."

"P arty" was an understatement for what Mrs. Granture had in mind. The backyard was transformed to fit enough tables and chairs to seat fifty people. In the center, shaded by an umbrella, was a long table with a black cloth over it to provide some "elegance," in her own words. Megan quickly called her out that the sheet had been locked away in the shed for two years. The table was buckling under the monstrous amount of food she'd been cooking in the three days prior.

She'd even hired out a small bouncy castle for the children. It appeared their mother cared more for catering to others than herself and the actual celebration for her birthday. The concept was somewhat foreign to me. I'd only ever known a mother who was selfish and cold. I found myself uncomfortable and almost envious of those who had this as their "normal."

Alex had migrated inside to get me another drink. I shrunk into the outer edge of the social gathering. Sure, work events no problem, I knew what to say and when to say it... but personal gatherings like this? Well, mingling had never been my strong suit.

Noticing my uncomfortableness, Hayden pulled himself away from the small circle of guests swooning around him and joined me. He was quite the little celebrity here it would appear.

"How are you holding up?" he asked.

"It's really nice."

He laughed as if sensing my discomfort. "I'd only been to two of Mrs. Granture's parties both of which were just as extravagant. I'm pretty sure she invites all the neighbors as well. Apparently, their father used to grumble about all the parties and dinners she hosted, but secretly loved them."

"Did you know their father well?" I asked.

"No, he'd passed away before I had the pleasure of meeting him," he said quietly.

I couldn't even remember mine. In my teens, I'd struggled with the notion of missing something I never had. As an adult, I'd simply bowed to the fact of having a shitty mother and no father.

"I'm curious about something," he trailed. "Completely not work related."

I side-eyed him, and he laughed.

"That's usually when you say, okay?" he prompted.

"Okay?"

"What's really going on between you and Alex?" he asked as he looked Alex's way.

Instead of remaining tight-lipped ignoring or denying it, I quipped back in response, "I could ask you the same about Clover's sister."

He whistled and blew out a breath. "She's sharp. I was not expecting that from you."

I smoothed over my blonde bob, slightly uncomfortable. *Damn it,* what was it about cocky, arrogant men that really had me breaking out of my composure.

"Sharp isn't necessarily bad by the way," he added gently. No, but it meant people were seeing through me and that *was* bad.

"How did I just know you were talking crap all the way from over there simply by recognizing that cocky smile of yours?" Megan waltzed over.

He defensively raised his hands. "Me, I would never," he teased, rolling his tongue in his cheek.

"Mom said you guys have to try this," Megan said, offering us both a plate of what looked like potato salad with a small amount of chili flakes on it.

"Oh, thank you." *Chilli.* I silenced my complaints.

"Do all the men in New York look like that?" Megan

asked pointedly in Alex's direction as he made his way through the crowd, a spark of jealousy rushing through me. A nauseating emotion I quickly pushed down.

"What do you have against Ithaca men?" Hayden whined. She shrugged in response.

"Here I got you some cake as well," Alex said, looking down at the plate in my hand. "Did you get that?"

"Umm no, Megan's mother suggested I try some," I said, hoping not to sound offensive.

"It looks delicious, let's swap," he charmed, giving me the cake instead. Relief rippled through me. Whether he remembered I was allergic to chilli or not, I was grateful to not have to appear ungrateful for the plate Megan offered to me. He also handed me one of the two glasses.

Megan pointed over to the food. "Oh, you don't have to share there's more than enough potato bake for everyone."

Ethan's shrill scream broke through the music and busy chatter. He'd landed in front of the bouncing castle, screaming and holding his arm as he rocked from side to side. A silence fell over everyone as they cleared her a path.

"Ethan!" Megan panicked. He was wailing in pain, clutching his arm. Megan assessed it within a moment, trying to bend and touch it. "It looks broken."

"I'll drive you to the hospital." Hayden was already on the move.

"Mom, you stay here. Clover, look after Mom," Megan instructed forcefully before carrying Ethan and leaving through the kitchen with Hayden only a few steps behind her.

"I'll check up on them," Damon promised Clover, then shadowed them. Everything happened so quickly.

Clover calmed her mother while other guests quickly rallied the children off the jumping castle, unsure. "It's okay, Mom. Megan had a broken arm too once, remember? He'll be okay," Clover encouraged. I stood there with cake in hand not sure where I was needed or what could be done.

Damon came through the kitchen, adjusting his light-blue business shirt. "They've taken him to the hospital. Let the doctors do what they do best," Damon said to Mrs. Granture with a reassuring smile and absentmindedly placing his hand on Clover's lower back. Again, they look so perfectly suited but felt so far away. How was I supposed to act around them outside of work? They weren't friends... I didn't really have need for those. "I broke my arm once falling off a horse. It sucked, but I thought I was really cool when all the kids signed my cast," Damon said, lightening the mood.

"I never knew that," Alex piped up, standing behind me. He'd become more casual around me, his proximity a mere breath away and I was no longer finding the same motive to push him away like I always felt the need to. Did it look as "right" between Alex and me as it looked for Clover and Damon? And that thought alone was terrifying, an unfamiliar chill running through my body.

"And besides, we don't know if it's definitely broken. He might've just fallen awkwardly," Clover added.

"It'll be okay," Damon reassured us, his expression so open and warm that in that moment, I couldn't believe anything else.

"How old were you when you fell off the horse?" Clover asked. He threw his head back, smiling as Clover's mother excused herself and attended to one of the guests recommending her potato salad.

"It's a long story." He laughed, embarrassed.

As if his laughter were contagious, she smiled, love filling her gaze. "I've got all day." And so with nowhere to go, he began to tell us the story about the pony, not a horse, who decided to throw an eight-year-old-Damon off at their local ranch. And amongst it all... I considered what it might be like to not be so alone. What would it feel like if I had a family and relationship like this? Was that even possible for me?

Chapter 22

Alex

Three hours later, Hayden, Megan, and Ethan returned. Megan put Ethan to bed in her room upstairs and came down after Hayden. He'd already grabbed a beer from the fridge and downed it, looking rather pale. Megan followed suit, grabbing a glass of wine. Sotiny had been gradually downing her drinks but I knew the lightweight would definitely be feeling it, considering how chatty she'd become in the last hour with strangers.

"How's Ethan?" Clover asked as she wrapped her arms around Damon's waist. The two looked good together. A small part of me was envious of that. Two weeks ago, it might've not bothered me as much. But all this time with Sotiny brought up old feelings. Unrequited ones. Especially after last night and how easily she brushed it off. I didn't know how to make sense of that. I didn't usually care about women's feelings in that regard and yet, I felt like I was the one being hidden away or disposed of.

"He'll be okay, but it's broken. He'll be tender for a while," Megan said, sounding drained. "I'll check up on him again in a minute and stay up there with him. Not as bad as this one though." She shrugged a shoulder Hayden's way.

Hayden gave her a sharp side-glance, taking another begrudging sip, some color slowly returning to his pale complexion.

"Looks like big-shot sports manager over here can't handle the look of disfigured bones or hospital wards," Megan teased, nudging him with her shoulder. Hayden looked like he wanted to say something but didn't.

"That's right," Clover said, looking as if she'd had a lightbulb moment. "You pass out at the smell of blood as well, don't you?"

He grimaced.

"The doctors at one point were more concerned about him falling on top of me than Ethan's arm," Megan laughed.

"It wasn't even that bad," Hayden sulked. "I just lost my footing is all." He looked down at his beer in disappointment. "Yea, this isn't going down too well. I might have to call it quits for today, sorry."

"Don't be a baby," Megan teased. "Come on, you can check up on Ethan with me and have a rest in there. Mom hasn't even cut the cake yet, you can recover by then. She would tear you apart if you left before you had your slice." Megan grabbed his ear and started pulling him toward the stairs. Much to my surprise, Hayden didn't argue.

I felt a heated gaze on me and looked around to find Sotiny's blue eyes immediately. She'd been watching me all evening with that calculating stare. For as much as I knew her, at times, I knew nothing at all in what she was thinking.

"Have your sister and Hayden always been that close?" Damon asked.

"Not that I can remember," Clover drawled out. "I'm surprised Hayden's tolerating Megan's brutality."

"Well, maybe brutality runs in the family," Damon taunted.

"Ha ha, very funny, Mr. Brogardt," Clover said, stomping on his foot.

I spotted Sotiny walking through the crowd. "Excuse me."

Up the carpeted stairs and at the end of the hall,

she leant against the wall, waiting for the second bathroom. She looked exhausted.

Something in a nearby partly ajar door caught her attention. With small steps, she moved closer curiously. Silently, I leant over her shoulder to peer into the room as well, the scent of jasmine filling my nostrils. Gratefully she didn't push me away, only continued to peer into the darkly lit room.

A snore carried through. The ceiling fan swept a cool breeze throughout the room. On the left side of the bed, Ethan was sound asleep, his white cast pinned to the blanket over him. Megan was holding his hand, seated awkwardly on the floor with her head resting on the bed. Next to Ethan—much to my amusement—was Hayden, who'd passed out with his top four buttons undone and a small bucket beside him.

I tried not to laugh out loud. He must've been feeling really sick if Megan cared enough to get him a bucket. And what an interesting side to see from the playboy self-made billionaire in the sports industry of all things, where I'd imagined he should've been desensitized to broken bones.

The toilet flushed and the sound of a running tap began. Guiltily, Sotiny and I spun around and casually leant against opposing walls as if we were up to nothing. One of the guests walked out, a curt nod as he left down the hallway.

"What are you doing here?" she asked.

"I just wanted to make sure you were alright."

"I'm okay, I just..." She wrapped her arms around herself insecurely.

"Wanted a breather for five minutes? There's a lot of people down there."

She said nothing but slowly she nodded. It was something. At least she wasn't pushing me away. Despite her efforts in New York, and inability for anyone else to notice otherwise, she preferred her own company. Events like this always took it out of her.

She scanned the empty hallway and then her gaze landed on me. Quietly, she said, "But I don't mind spending time with *you*. In there..." Her gaze darted to the bathroom.

Whatever restraint I'd managed up until this point snapped. I scooped her up against the wall, rolling my tongue against hers as we clumsily pivoted around the doorframe and into the room. I slammed her against the door shoving my hand under her bra and pinching her nipples. Her head leaned back, a small moan escaping before she cupped her mouth.

"Sshh," she reminded me, even though it was her

who made the noise. She chuckled, pressing gentle kisses down my neck. I growled, that small tender moan of hers belonging to me. My dick was rock-hard. I lifted her by her ass, my grip firm enough to leave bruising marks as I plopped her onto the bench. With her quick hands and help, I pulled down her pants and underwear and shoved her back against the cold tiled wall.

She hissed. "Fuck it's cold." But her complaints melted away as I furled my tongue around her clit, flicking back and forth like a starved man. I delved my tongue deep inside of her, eating her out like she was my salvation and last breath. My cock was painfully hard against the zip of my pants, throbbing to be inside of her.

"Alex," she moaned again. "I want you to fuck me so bad."

So many years I'd wanted her to say that, more times than I could count. I dipped two fingers in her, satisfied by the sharp hiss that crept out of her. I kissed her selfishly, swallowing those pleading little moans.

"If you haven't been with any other men, then how do you please yourself, baby girl," I asked, finger fucking her as she became increasingly wet.

She seemed incoherent, her head and eyes

rolling in the back of her head as she gripped the bathroom counter. I bit her neck, marking what was mine again. She hissed, her other hand and nails painfully raking down my back. "Tell me, sweet, sweet girl, what gets that pussy soaking wet."

"I use toys," she breathed harshly, a heavy admission. I growled. The image of this beautiful creature fucking herself into oblivion had me ridiculously rock-hard. I wanted to fist her hair and fuck her, ruining her for any other man that might try to look at her twice.

I bit her again, pulling back skin. "Ow," she hissed.

I stopped. Shit was I too rough for her?

"Don't stop," she moaned. "I like it. All of this. All of you."

A flash of vulnerability waved over her. She pulled me back to her lips, small moans escaping into my mouth as I slid a third finger inside of her.

"Tell me what else you like," I purred into her mouth, the swell of my cock ridiculously painful.

She incoherently moaned. I bit her lip and tugged. Liking it when she did the same to me. "Tell me what you like, baby girl."

With a lucid consideration, she said, "I want you to stick a finger up my ass."

I arched a brow. "Really?"

Sotiny might've been a virgin but that made her no less a filthy girl and a demand I was happy to oblige.

Tapping that rattled against the door had us both freezing. After a split second, coherency returned, recalling where we were. I tilted my head toward the door. "Yes?" I said, still knuckle deep in Sotiny. She blanched, hiding her red face in her hands.

"Oh, sorry I wasn't sure if someone was in there, I can wait," an elderly woman echoed from the hallway.

I pressed my forehead to Sotiny's shoulder, defeated.

"We can't," Sotiny reasoned. "Maybe we can finish this in the car on the way home?" She arched a promiscuous eyebrow.

My cock throbbed at the idea. I kissed her gently on the corner of her lips and placed my hands on either side of her, locking her in.

"You and that filthy mouth of yours is driving me into a madman, baby girl."

She kicked up a smile.

"Then you'll have no issues fucking me in that car you love oh so much."

I considered her. "I'm not going to fuck you in

the car, Sotiny." A frown crossed her expression, confusion and hurt marring her features. "When we get back to New York, I want to take you on a proper date and then bring you back to mine. I don't want this to be some weekend fun you decided to have and then as soon as we're back in the office you clam up and run away again. I want to have a proper go of this."

She seemed confused, and I could sense that guard slowly creeping up again. I grabbed her hand and kissed her knuckles gently. "There won't be any other women. Just you and me."

She seemed affronted. "What more do you want from me? Isn't this what you were after?"

"I want you, baby girl, and I thought that was perfectly clear. No running away or hiding. We do this properly. And if you decide still after a few months, it's not what you want..." I swallowed, unsure of what promises I was making. "I'll agree to sign the divorce papers."

Confusion marred her face and as if reading her, I added, "I'm all in to try and make this work. It's up to you."

She considered me for a while, too long because my next breath hinged on her reply. With a gentle tone, she said, "Then we need some rules around this."

"Whatever you like."

She pushed me back and fumbled to pull her pants back up, she smoothed over her blonde bob, that sharp intellect in her eyes rolling over me all businesslike again. "Rule one. No one's allowed to know at work."

I agreed.

"Rule two. We trial it *only* for a month and then after that we'll discuss how we feel about the situation and the trajectory as to whether this can be anything at all."

I smirked. Wow she really had a way of turning something so sincere into some business arrangement.

"Alex?" she prompted with hand on hip.

"I agree," I said with a smile. "What's your next rule, baby girl?"

"Rule three. You better fuck me so good it's a month I'll never forget."

Chapter 23

Sotiny

One day until I was back at the office didn't give me hardly enough time to prepare the mixed emotions I had in regards to a certain playboy. Alex and I agreed to one month. But I wasn't entirely sure what that might entail. I'd never gone on dates or had a fling. And despite my burning desire to fuck him in Ithaca, I was becoming more anxious the longer I had to wait and think about it.

I chewed on my thumbnail waiting for my coffee to be called out in our local café. Memories of our weekend rushed toward me every spare moment I seemed to have. I'd used my vibrator and eggs on myself multiple times yesterday and none of it remotely took the edge off. Which was infuriatingly disturbing.

The bell jingled as someone stepped into the café, and as if summoned by the mere thought, I was staring right at Alex's cocky smile, creating a dimple. I looked away, my heart fluttering. Why did he have such a boyish effect on me? I was a woman in her thirties dammit. Surely, I shouldn't be feeling like a teenager.

"Alex!" the barista flirted. "How was your trip away in Ithaca?"

"It was really good, I really think we made some progress," he said, looking over his shoulder, his gaze dropping to the deep blue scarf tightly wrapped around my neck. I touched it self-consciously. The three bruising marks he'd given me in the span of two nights couldn't be completely covered by concealer. And despite my irritation that he'd left them there, I'd also dazed at them longingly thinking about how they'd happened.

With hands resting in his jacket pockets, he stood beside me casually. "That's a nice scarf."

"Yes, well I'd much prefer it if I could take it off at some point today, however due to being branded by some animal, I don't have much of a choice," I gritted out.

His chuckle flooded warmth to my core. "I'm sure that animal heard no complaints at the time. Ironically you should see the claw marks down my back. Someone might think I was mauled by a bear."

I smoothed over my hair, refusing to let the embarrassment show on my face.

"You didn't reply to my last text message yesterday." he inquired.

My eyebrows knitted together in confusion. "It wasn't a question."

He seemed taken aback. "Does it have to be a question for you to keep a conversation going?"

"I find texting annoying."

"You don't exactly thrive off talking to people in person either," he pointed out.

"True." I searched the room, certain someone would overhear our conversation or learn about our dirty secret. I didn't want to be the next office affair that others spoke about. I didn't want anyone to look or think about me twice. I reiterated, "Rule number one—"

"No one in the office can find out. I know, Sots. This is our little secret," he said casually, still watching our coffees being made. "You look beautiful today by the way."

My breath hitched, the customary reaction to say

something snide in return bubbling up. I pushed it down. Plenty had called me beautiful, but it never meant much to me. Not unless it came out of his mouth. "Thank you."

"Yours is ready to go, Sotiny," Regine, the café owner, sang out. "By the way I like your scarf."

"Thank you." I smiled timidly and collected the tray of two coffees. One for me and one for Michelle.

"See you around?" Alex remarked as I headed for the door.

"Sure." I was betting on it.

By the time I'd reached Michelle's office, I was already in a fluster. Cold dread ran through me. What had I agreed to? What if people discovered our relationship? I'd been avoiding it for years so now wouldn't it only attract more attention if they spot us talking?

When I walked into Michelle's office, she was hunched over her chair with a bin in her lap.

"Are you okay?" I asked, closing the door behind me. Surely, she didn't want anyone seeing her in this state. I plopped the tray of coffees down.

"I'm fine. At least I was until ten minutes ago." She took a slow breath. I stood in front of her awkwardly, unsure as to what to do.

She leaned back in her chair, looking awfully

pale. "I don't think you should be in today." I commented.

She raised her eyebrows, as if it were a good idea. She'd now been in this state for weeks.

"Nothing from the doctors?" I asked.

"Nothing they can help with at the moment, apparently." She offered a small, defeated smile.

She pulled out some mouth spray, spraying her mouth. "I see the week in Ithaca was a success. And I heard you went to Clover's mother's birthday. How was that?"

Immediate flashes of Alex's torso and abs came to mind. Shared kisses and filthy words. "It was interesting," I coolly said. "Her nephew fell off a jumping castle and broke his arm. Turns out the big sports manager we hired, isn't too good with blood."

Michelle laughed before abruptly stopping and clutching to the bin as if it were her life support. She breathed through it.

"I really don't think you should be here today."

She glumly nodded her head. "I feel bad that you've been picking up a lot of the slack in my absence."

"And that's exactly why you hired me," I said, gathering the few things she'd unpacked and packing it back for her. "You need rest, Michelle."

She offered a polite smile. "I'll be sad when you move on. I might even offer a competitive bonus to make you consider staying."

"No one ever said I was going anywhere any time soon."

She considered that. "I forwarded your resume and recommendation to my friend. I imagine she'll be in touch real soon."

My heart froze, my slight pause as I packed her things noticed by Michelle. "You sent it already?"

"I'm a woman of my word. Now I better check in with Damon and let him—" She held up her hand, reaching for the bin.

I turned around. "I'll speak with Damon and call the driver to come and collect you." Once she'd finished barfing, a sight to behold in her branded maroon suit, I added, "We've got it all under control here. You can take some time off and well-deserved rest."

She'd inherited the majority of the tasks of the CEO when Damon was allegedly going through a personal matter. I never dove into it but as Amber had educated me, it was around some scandal with his ex. But now that he was back, more than ever over the past few months, Michelle had a team she could depend on. Including me. It almost felt bittersweet how quickly she'd applied for the role on my behalf and with a personal recommendation which I was certain to guarantee me an interview. And yet it all felt so sudden; I hadn't had time to mentally prepare myself for it.

And yet a bubble of excitement raced through me.

Damon's door was already open and by the laughing, I knew Alex was also inside. "Please if we were to get serious about boxing, I'd kick your ass," Alex joked. "You're just lucky I take it easy on you in the ring."

"Remind me what happened in March?"

"Pfft that black eye was nothing and I was hungover," Alex defended himself.

"Correction, you were still drunk and too slow to hold the pads properly. And in my defense, you also stepped into it."

"Stepped into your fist?" Alex threw back his head and laughed.

I knocked on the door. Both of them looked up bemused. In hindsight, it still seemed so offhanded to work with such attractive men. They both looked as if they'd stepped off the cover of a magazine, not run it. "Michelle's had to take her leave early today."

Damon went sullen. "She's sick again?"

I nodded.

"They still don't have any results?" Alex asked, the mood dampening.

Damon shook his head.

"She's left me with her schedule. Whatever meetings you can fill in for would be fantastic, Damon, but whatever's left I can take over and will report any decisions you might need to make."

"I appreciate that, Sotiny, I'll look over her schedule now. Also, nice scarf, I don't think I've seen you wear them very often."

A cold chill ran down my spine. I kept my gaze on Damon, refusing to look at Alex in case it gave away every little detail as to why I was wearing this scarf. Had he somehow seen us leaving the bathroom together at the party?

"Thank you. I felt like a little change with it getting colder and all. I'll be in my office if you need me." Relief swept through me as I put distance between us. He might've been good at acting casually, but I was realizing I, however, was terrible at it.

Two hours had passed and everyone else had flooded the office. I rescheduled meetings and replied to emails from the weekend on Michelle's behalf. My office was small, but at least my own. I'd been grateful that I didn't have to share space with anyone else; I often found it draining when people tried small talk constantly with me.

A light tap on the door grabbed my attention. A delivery man stood at my door. "I have a package here for Miss Sotiny Bryer."

Confused, I signed for the package—a white square box with a black ribbon and a neatly written tag on it.

Looking around the main office and onlookers, I took it into my room. Undoing the bow and pulling off the lid, I gaped at the delicately placed deep-blue lingerie. The see-through bra connected with a bejewelled neck piece that wrapped around the throat. The thong and garter were also bejewelled similarly. A small golden-sprayed rose sat inside on top of the white silk cloth it was propped on. Beside it was a small white note rimmed with a black glossy frame.

I'll pick you up on Friday at eight. – A

My mind went into overdrive. *How did he even*

get my sizing right? Because he'd been with that many women, I criticized. No, I wasn't comparing myself to the other women he'd been with.

I pulled out my cell and took a snap. I sent it to him with a quick message.

Looks like you have some competition, I don't know which of my many suitors sent this to me. But I wonder if I'll wear it...

Chapter 24

Sotiny

I wore a knitted beige dress, my long green coat complimenting the polarity of the colors. I'd curled my hair into small waves, something I infrequently did, and put some soft beige lip gloss on. I made sure to always look nice and presentable but definitely fretted more than I'd like to admit as to how I looked tonight.

When Alex buzzed in, I quickly threw a few things into my clutch and slipped on my heels. By the time I was ready, he was already knocking on the door.

I opened it and by way of greeting, said, "You know I could've met you downstairs."

His lips landed on mine, breaking any train of thought. His tongue brushed against mine, encouraging and demanding. A greeting without words. *I missed you.*

When he finally pulled back and I found myself hinging and leaning forward for more, he swiped at his lips. "Nice lip gloss." He cocked a smile.

"Well, it had been," I said breathlessly, grabbing for my clutch to reapply it. Alex was wearing dark denim jeans, a black shirt and leather jacket.

"You don't have to wear your scarf today?" he pointed out. My hand automatically flung to my neck.

"Well no, for the most part those little bites you left have covered up."

A small disapproving noise crept through. "Well, looks like I'll have to amend that."

Warmth spread to my lower stomach. "That's rather presumptuous, isn't it?"

He cocked one eyebrow, his smirk forming that singular dimple in his cheek. Did he really have to be so ridiculously good looking? "Are you wearing the gift I sent you?"

"Oh, was that from you?" I casually said, shrugging my shoulder. "I can't remember, I might've left it in the bottom of my closet, I think."

"Funny."

"Very," I deadpanned.

He offered his arm out to me. "Come along, Miss Granger, I believe we have a date."

I ignored the nickname I'd usually bite back on.

"Where are we going?" I asked curiously. What did an actual date look like to Alex? I had no idea what it looked like to me, but I'd read enough romances to have a broad spectrum. Theoretically anyways. None of them were titled the thirty-one-year-old woman who had never gone on a date let alone had sex with a man. No that would've been humiliating. *What a call card*, I thought sarcastically to myself.

"You look beautiful tonight," he said, his gaze scanning over me from head to toe.

"You pull up alright yourself," I commented.

"Tiffany is that you?" Winston my neighbor called out. He was two doors down. Always got my name wrong and was kind of loopy. "You're damn dog got out again and peed on my floor."

"No, not me. I don't own a dog, Winston."

"Don't you go lying, it's not in good taste." He threw a stubby finger at me. "I'll report ya."

"I'll be better next time." I politely smiled. I dug my nails into Alex's arm, knowing too well he'd try to step in on my behalf.

"And did you report to the building manager you've got a boy staying witcha?"

"I don't have a boy staying with me, Winston. Have a good night."

Miraculously, the elevator door opened with perfect timing. Only being on the second floor I often found it faster to use the stairs, but as luck would have it, not today. The lady from the fourth apartment on our floor held bags of groceries in her hands, yelling into her head piece what she described as her "deadshit girlfriend."

We squeezed into the elevator, waiting for the silence to finally envelop us. Carefully, Alex said, "Is it always this..." He chose his next word carefully. "Lively?"

"Loud?"

"Yea. How do you get any sleep?" he asked.

"It's not so bad," I added as we stepped out of the building. I pointed into the direction of the road-works that had been happening over the last eight months. "And I have my personal alarm outside my window when they start at five every morning."

Alex's features twisted. "I don't even think that's legal."

"It's Manhattan, it's always loud, isn't it?"

And to that he couldn't deny.

"Where are we going?" I couldn't spot his car. I always found it strange that locals had their own cars but found it easier to use cabs to get around town, especially for parking. A sleek black car waited for us, the driver stepping out and opening the door for me.

"It's a surprise," Alex said, then walked around the other side.

Nervous flutters aroused in my stomach as I picked at my clutch.

"You've been quiet at work," Alex noted.

"No more than usual."

"I thought, you might talk to me a bit more."

I chuckled. "Did you think we'd be having secret rendezvous in the closet, Alex?" I bit my bottom lip and he looked surprised. I was always at the office early and late, as if I hadn't caught Clover and Damon taking deliberate time in small spaces around the office.

"No of course, I'd hate to think anything was double-booked," he charmed. "But you know you can talk to me a little more in the office."

"Are you lonely, Alex? I never expected you as the needy type?"

"Needy?" he choked. "I'm not. I'm not needy. That's just normal when people admit they're into each other they make more time for one another. I think."

I stared down at my clutch. "Ah. It's not that I hadn't thought about talking to you. But then I wasn't sure what we'd talk about. And then people around the office might be suspicious that we're speaking voluntarily together considering we've never usually been so, you know, easygoing?"

Alex laughed, grabbing my hand and rubbing his thumb over considerately. "We'll take this at your pace, Sotiny. But you don't ever have to worry about what we'll talk about or how. Just like this now, it's perfect. It doesn't have to be about anything in particular."

That made sense. I really wasn't any good at this stuff.

"At your own pace, Sotiny. It always will and it always has been. I can be a patient man."

I side-eyed his profile. He looked like he'd just come off some TV set or studio. How was this still the same Alex? Where he'd grown, I felt like I was still held back as that teenager I was around him. I didn't even shine a torch beside him, and yet he was taking me out. I tried to push away the insecurities, frustrated that only in my work I felt any confidence whatsoever.

"We're here," Alex said with a smile as we pulled up on the curb.

"Central Park?" I said curiously.

"When was the last time you were here?" he asked rhetorically. "I'm making a bet at best, you've only been here once since living here, if that. At worst you've only seen the space of your apartment, grocery store, the office and stretching out to a local library now and then to keep it spicy?"

My mouth went wide, and I stuttered, "I've been places."

"Oh really? How many times have you been to Central Park?"

Prompted by my silence, he smiled and dragged me out of the car.

"I've never done this either, so it should be fun." He pointed to the carriage of horses.

I stopped dead in my tracks. "We're going in that?"

"Yea." He seemed nervous all of a sudden. "I remember you once talking about wanting to go horse riding. I know it's not the same but if you don't want to, we don't have to. Shit, now that I think about it, is this a bad idea?"

I chuckled. "I've never seen you like this, Alex."

"Like what?" he growled.

"Nervous." I pressed a kiss to his cheek, the natural feel and movement in it surprising even me. Everything about Alex felt comfortable and right. But that was a reality check I'd face at the end of the month. "And I love the idea. Thank you."

"Good. Give me one second," he darted off to a nearby cart and came back with two hot chocolates. "Don't worry it's skim."

It immediately warmed up my hands. He spoke to the carriage driver. It was ridiculously ornate, dripping in ribbon and fake flowers. Alex stepped up first, grabbing my hand to help me up. We sat pressed against one another. Both my hands were strapped to the hot chocolate. This felt strange and my stomach kept somersaulting, much like when I used to see him as a teenager. It felt odd to think of the fifteen-year-old crush turning into our first date sixteen years later.

"How did you know I haven't seen much of the sights?" I asked quietly, taking a sip of the hot chocolate and admiring the night life of Central Park. So many people were still out—walking their dogs, couples strolling hand in hand, joggers, and performers keeping the paths alive.

"I don't know if you realize this, Sots, but you're one of the biggest introverts I know."

"Well, I don't think I'd ever labeled it. And how does this work for you, party boy? Friday night by now you'd be 'hitting the town.' How does it feel to be casually strolling through Central Park on a carriage pulled by horse?"

His smile kicked up slightly. "I'm elated." My heart skipped its next beat.

I took another mouthful of my hot chocolate. "I'm glad to hear."

He chuckled, enjoying his own mouthful before pulling my attention to the small group of acrobats. I gawked in astonishment, amazed by their peculiar ability. Sure, I was flexible from yoga... but not that flexible.

I pointed to the artist who painted with a small light over his canvas. It was a completely different world here. Full of life and people enjoying their Friday evening. Just as I was. And I had Alex to thank for that.

Chapter 25

Alex

I'd reserved a French restaurant on Park Avenue for dinner. It offered a fine cuisine in an aesthetically charming space.

Sotiny swept her sharp gaze over the restaurant, the hint of a smile indicating her pleasure. I let out a satisfied breath I hadn't even realized I'd been holding onto. I'd never put this much thought into a date. Even the horse and carriage was a gamble. If Damon saw me in this state right now, he'd give me a hard time for sure. Especially considering how much crap I'd given him by way of his balls being cut off since dating Clover.

The waiter collected our coats and led us to our table, suggesting their house champagne to start with. We ordered two glasses and he left us with the menu.

"It's beautiful in here," Sotiny commented, looking over her menu and at me. Male pride filled me.

"It is," I remarked, insinuating her.

She dropped her head back to the menu. I chuckled. She always shied away from compliments. How so much of her hadn't changed.

"Two glasses," our waiter chimed, placing them down. "Do you know what you'll be having to eat?"

I waited for Sotiny to order first.

"I'll have the salmon, please."

"And I'll have the filet mignon. Can we grab a side of bread and salad of greens with that too please."

"Of course." The waiter smiled politely and took our menus.

"I hope you already know what you want for dessert," I asked, holding out my hand. With little resistance, she slid her small palm into mine, almost is if contemplating its ease. Baby steps.

"The crème brûlée of course," she commented with a sweet smile.

"I was looking at the poached pear. Two great minds think alike."

"But we're ordering different things," she said, dipping her head on the side in confusion. I liked this side to her. The one she'd only let me see. Past the cold and busy exterior was this woman who needed to be brought out of her shell inch by inch.

"Exactly. Now we can try both."

She laughed and said rather smugly before taking a sip of champagne, "Who said I was going to share?"

"You're not going to force me to bend you over and spank your pretty little ass in front of all these people, are you?"

She choked on her mouthful of champagne. I chuckled, smug with her response.

"Just when I thought you were being well-behaved," she quietly said, searching the room, obviously making sure no one else heard.

"I think you prefer me when I'm not," I said, rubbing over her thumb considerately. "I want you to tell me what it is you want me to do to you tonight."

She seemed taken aback and bit her bottom lip. With a quiet and skeptical tone, she asked, "Right here?"

"Yes, baby girl." I wanted her out of that shell of hers. Because damn, when she spoke dirty, it turned me on.

She bit at her bottom lip before taking another swig. "I want you to fuck me tonight, Alex." She combed back her hair, like she always did when she was nervous or uncomfortable. I was willing to accept that as an answer for now. I'd made it my personal mission to see how filthy I could make this girl within the month. To bring out that wild little vixen that she'd hidden away for all these years.

Chapter 26

Sotiny

I wasn't sure what to expect from Alex's apartment, but this wasn't it. I knew he'd come a long way and set himself up. I just didn't realize how much. Polished wooden floors created depth against the dark-blue lounges, ceiling-high windows adorned the living room, showcasing the beautiful dazzling city backdrop.

On the right was the kitchen and what appeared to be a bedroom and bathroom. On the left and down a hallway looked to be another room and second living space, containing a bar and pool table. The stairs beside the wooden double-door entrance to the second living area lead into a loft with city views and a king-sized bed. I assumed the small room beside it was the bathroom and a walk-in closet.

The apartment itself was edgy and the type of fine architecture I'd never seen in someone's home, only ever in magazines. Well except for Michelle's home but I wasn't expecting something so refined from Alex.

"Alex you *own* this?" He shrugged. "And an apartment in Chicago and Los Angeles. I'm looking at some real estate in Seattle or San Francisco next."

"I didn't realize you were into real estate," I commented, looking over the small inbuilt wooden bookshelf and his selection. All of them were nonfiction, the complete opposite to my own collection.

"Would you like a glass of wine?" Alex asked, looking over the wooden shelving of mixed wines. He grabbed two glasses from the rack beside it.

"Do you have red?" I asked. I still couldn't get over the size of this apartment. "And what's this painting about?" I asked staring up at the painting that took up the majority of his living room. I noticed no television in sight.

He walked over, offering me a glass and stared at it for a while. Simultaneously, we cocked our heads to one side. "Honestly, I still have no idea. I drunk bid on it at one of the auctions Damon dragged me to once. At least the money went to charity I suppose."

"Such a noble man you are," I added.

"Or just learnt a powerful lesson not to attend auctions while drinking copious amounts of champagne. I'm certain they only give free champagne so suckers like me bid recklessly."

I laughed walking up the stairs to the loft and into the main bedroom, eyes drawn to the king-sized bed, then peeped through the bathroom to the claw bath house big enough to fit two.

"Remind me what you did before coming to New York again?"

He chuckled taking a mouthful. "I might've made some lucky investments."

But I knew that were only half the truth. Despite his playboy ways it was his only fault, if one could class it that. Being hired at *Be True* as head of their marketing wasn't a small feat, not forgetting to mention all the start-up business he'd established and maintained during his career already. A small pang of guilt ran through me. I'd been so hard on him all this time, simply because of his womanizing ways and yet in every other way he'd grown up and matured. He'd established stability around him. At best I'd found a small apartment to live in temporarily until I was off to the next place.

He crept up behind me, his hands curling around my waist and resting on my lower stomach.

He rested his chin on the dip between my neck and shoulder. My core tightened, the simple heat off him flaring up my entire back.

"Do you know how many times I've thought about you in this apartment?" he asked.

I froze under his honesty. Now that we'd called a truce, it was more difficult to speak the truth than hide behind the lies. I'd for so long thought about being in his arms like this but was it really okay for me to ever admit that out loud?

I twisted around to face him. Although I couldn't say how I felt, I could show him. I plucked his glass out of his hand and placed them both onto the side table. I shoved him back onto the bed, a slight nervousness arousing within me. It was exhilarating yet terrifying all at once. When I was with Alex, I felt most myself. That despite all my ugliness that I hid, he saw the *real* me and still wanted to stay. And yet my inexperience didn't escape me.

But confidently and slowly, I pulled my dress over my chest, wiggled it over my hips, and dropped it to the floor. He stared at me, the flash of city lights silhouetting his broad shoulders. Those green eyes were as dark as a forest at night, but potently filled with lust as he watched me.

Silently, I was at his command just as much as he

was at mine. But I wanted to give myself to him like this. My final admission to stepping into whatever this one-month thing was.

"How'd you guess my measurements?" I asked, running my hand along my body, showcasing the bedazzled lingerie set he'd bought me.

He licked his lips, the thickness in his pants swelling. "Because I've watched you every day since you've walked into that office building with those tight pencil skirts of yours and blouse that covers everything—leaving it all to fucking imagination."

My stomach filled with what felt like butterflies, a chill creeping over my skin.

"Come here," he demanded. Quietly, I walked over to him, the slight tap of my heels the only noise to come between us.

I grabbed his hands, tracing them over my smooth skin and hips. His gaze trailed every dip and curve I led him over. He was hungry, his eyes a maddening and yet satisfying thing to see.

"I'm only going to ask you one more time, Sotiny, are you sure about this?"

Slowly, I placed one knee up on either side of him, straddling him, satisfied by the thick bulge that rubbed against my lace panties. "I haven't been more certain of anything else in my life."

Of course I wanted to lose my virginity, especially to Alex. But that didn't make me some holy maiden. I pushed him back, kneeling over with him to lie on top. I kissed him, nibbling at his bottom lip and dragging it out. He growled, the sound vibrating through me.

His hand brushed over the lingerie and my stomach, wrapping around to my ass and squeezing hard. He twisted slightly, a painful kind of pleasure racing through me.

He rolled us over until I was on my back. Gently, he pressed a kiss to my heart before trailing small bites down my stomach and to the lace panties.

"Should I take my heels off?" I asked, not letting the nervousness show. I'd hardly drunk tonight and for some reason it made the situation far more nerve-wracking and embarrassing.

"Leave them on," he growled.

I tried to steady my breathing. Thoughtfully, he pushed himself up and away. "What are you doing?"

"What would you like to do to me first, baby girl?"

Butterflies scattered in my stomach. *He was giving me control.* Gratefully, and far more at ease with it, I licked my lips. "I want you take those pants off."

At my command, he did. His cock sprang free, the size of it forcing me to take an involuntary gulp. And yet, my whole body felt alive, on fire even.

"Firstly, I want to suck on you while you admire the gift you bought me."

A small growl his reply. Licking my lips, I took him into my mouth. Further and further, I let him slide until I reluctantly gagged as it hit the back of my throat. Pushing past that, I tried to take all of him. I wanted all of him inside of me in every way. To be able to please him and ensure my inexperience was not so obvious. Sure, I'd watched a descent amount of porn, all of it only giving me an idea as to what I should do to please him.

I kept sucking, licking, and tasting every part of him, tears pricking my eyes. The simple pleasure of pleasing him sent sparks through me, my stomach unfurling with greed and heat.

His hand grabbed the back of my hair, thrusting me further onto his cock. I grabbed both sides of his ass, my nails digging in and clawing at him like I could take more.

The satisfying taste of precum hit the back of my throat, that small pulse in his veiny cock eliciting a bolt of electricity through me. All control snapped. I looked up into his green eyes. As if knowing, he pulled himself out and kissed me so hard, I was certain I'd bruise.

He slid his fingers into my panties, circling around my clit. "Shit, you're soaking wet, baby girl."

"You make me ridiculously horny," I breathed. "And I haven't forgotten or forgiven you for all those times you left me... unsatisfied."

A low warning growl rippled through him. He grabbed my throat, the hard press of his palm almost enough to cut off my breathing, but not quite. Fear and excitement slithered through me. "Then you're not leaving this apartment until you're *satisfied.*"

"Yes," I breathed. His lips came crashing down on mine as he worked the bud of my nerves, my legs shaking tenderly. He dipped a finger and then two into me, pumping me for all I was worth.

I dragged my nails down his back and bit into his shoulder, the same way he'd done to me. A tendril popped out of his neck as he moaned. His other hand twisted my ass, his rock-hard cock pinned against my stomach. That tender pain and arousal blurred lines I hadn't ever experienced or known.

He stepped away from the bed and to his drawer where he pulled out a condom packet. My breath hitched. *This was happening.* He efficiently ripped the edge of the packet off with his teeth. I watched him put it on, nervous and aroused all the same.

"Lay down, baby girl," he commanded. I did as he said, every part of my body feeling as if it was rigidly creaking one vertebrae at a time. "We'll take this slow."

I shook my head nervously. For all my talk and eagerness to be here, I was nervous. Could it be that different from my toys? That was preparation enough, right? I'd talked such a big game and pretended like I knew what I was doing but what if it was different? Shit what if I bled? What if I didn't like it and it wasn't what I fantasised at all?

"Sotiny," Alex said, bringing me back to the room and carefully hovering over me. "It's okay."

"I know," I breathed. Gently, he pressed a kiss to my lips. A slow and reassuring reminder that I was with him here, now. That I was okay. That we would be okay and that this felt right. My tangle of nerves dampened, preoccupied and focused by that heavy heat and thrumming that pounded at my core.

Slowly, with both hands, he pulled down my panties, kissing down my legs until he flicked them off and over my heels. He slowly trailed up again, that featherlight touch sending chills up my body.

His lips found mine again, that wicked tongue of

his alluring, possessive, and demanding more from me than I'd ever known possible. My body moved of its own accord, my knees squeezing together in anticipation. Was there any way this fire could be put out?

He growled as my nails dug into his back again and satisfyingly, I could see the markings I'd left on his throat.

"Open up for me, baby girl," he breathed against my lips. At his command, I opened my legs further. He rubbed his cock against my entrance; I squirmed beneath him, thrilled and on fire.

Slowly he nudged his size in and fuck me was it painful. A sharp sting sparked as he slowly rolled into me little by little.

"Breath, baby girl," he said. I hadn't even noticed my hitched breath. Those dark, lust-filled, forest-green eyes stared at me. Lost in them, I remembered why I was here. With Alex. This was always his to take. My whole body seemed to fall into a stupor, melting into him. No guards. No resistance. Just us.

He slid in further, the pain not emanating as deeply anymore. He nearly pulled out before pushing back in again. The motions slowly picking up in rhythm as a completely different kind of pleasure rushed over me. Around the tenderness, my core began to build like a dam.

I pulled his face to mine, kissing him, needing some kind of reassurance that he felt the same.

His thrusts sped up, his massive arm hovering over us as he held onto the wooden headboard as it knocked against the wall. I was jolted beneath it, a satisfied moan bubbling out of me involuntarily.

He grabbed me around the throat, that thrill and fear jolting through me as my pussy stretched so widely around him. Everything around us was lost. I curled my legs around his hips, the change in position creating a wave of pain and then pleasure all in one. "Fuck me," I breathed, going doe-eyed as I tried to focus on Alex.

His grip tightened around my throat as he pounded into me, that rising sensation clambering to such a build, I thought I'd fall off at any time.

"Alex," I stuttered. "I think I'm going to come."

He bit my bottom lip, the electricity of it jolting through me as everything gave way and I screamed his name as a powerful wave passed through me.

With a final thrust and grunt, he came inside of me. My pussy pulsed around him, tightening and squeezing the subtle jerk of him, leaving us sated.

Holy shit. My vibrator had never prepared me for that.

His grip loosened around my throat as he dropped his forehead to mine.

Those green eyes looked sated, his bulging neck muscles red and flustered.

"Thank you," I whispered, ridiculously content to stay like this forever. I didn't even want to move. Probably couldn't move. I slowly unpeeled my legs from around his waist as he pulled out.

In reply, he pressed his lips to mine, gentler this time. Soothing even. A whole new wave of endearment took hold, as again we conveyed what we felt with words unsaid. Only his body and mine. Only us.

Chapter 27

Alex

I'd scooped her off the bed and into the hot soaking bath, pressing in behind her. She lazily leant back against my chest, the bottom of her hair soaking. She looked like a satisfied cat, sleepy and yawning as she played with the water in front of her.

"How do you feel?" I asked, rubbing soap over her, cleaning her shoulders.

"Like I know you and I don't," she admitted, looking over her shoulder at me. "How long have we known one another for? What, twenty years? And I know we haven't spoken for all of that time, but I thought I knew exactly who you were. But these past few weeks, I'm learning so many different things about you. It's just surprising is all."

"Well, you know that tends to happen when you lay down your sword and have a conversation with someone." I curled my hands around her and squeezed playfully.

"You know why we couldn't talk," she said quietly.

Of course I knew why.

That night in Vegas had destroyed anything and everything between us. A drunken mistake. And yet one I couldn't entirely regret. That piece of signed paper floating somewhere was the last thing that linked us. Selfishly, I knew it would be the reason she'd find herself on my doorstep again, most likely because she wanted to marry some stable perfect guy. *Over my dead body.*

"Did you know I was transferring to *Be True*?" she asked.

"Yes," I admitted. "It came up in discussion and of course I recognized your name."

"And you had nothing to do with the recruiting?" She continued playing with the water.

"We've discussed this already haven't we, Sots? Why don't you think your portfolio was enough?"

She went quiet.

"You've always been more than enough," I added, praying that she didn't lash out me for it.

How else would someone who was raised to believe they were worthless and a burden think? And although she'd changed and grown a lot, I wondered how much that taunted her behind that beautiful polished shell of hers.

"You're the only one who's ever really seen me," she said quietly.

I held her tightly, resting my chin on her head. Her fingers brushed back and forth over my forearm.

And not that I had any complaints. I didn't want any other man to see her for the beautiful temperamental creature she was. But the only one holding her back was herself. "You can be seen, beautiful girl, if only you'll let others in."

But selfishly, I only asked that she at least let me in because I wasn't the type to share, as I was recently discovering about myself. Paper or not, Sotiny Bryer was mine.

Chapter 28

Sotiny

"And why do you think you'd be best suited for this role, Miss Bryer?" Susanna, the editor in chief, asked. Sitting on screen beside her during the online meeting was their recruiting manager.

"I bring a wide range of skillsets and a passion for books since as long as I can remember. Everything I've ever done has always been to acquire a role such as this. I'm quite grateful that Michelle Brogardt has been kind enough to organise an interview with you."

"Maybe so but it's your resume that got you here. Regarding your skillset it's rather versatile indeed. You've had so many jobs over the last few years that I question your intention of longevity here."

Ah. An anticipated question. One, as embarrassing as it might've been, I could only answer honestly. I opened my mouth and closed it again. This was the interview I'd been waiting for all my life and I didn't want to give the wrong answer. A tightness constricted in my throat. I resisted the urge to brush over my hair.

"Being entirely transparent, everything I did in my early twenties has been to afford going through college and thereafter. I found financial hardship in the few internships I took on and later was put in a situation to financially support my family. It wasn't until I was given this role at *Be True* and on its wage that I've been able to sustain myself. It's not that I lack in skills or drive, or the desire to have stability in my job. It was simply at the time it wasn't possible for me."

I could feel the bobble in my throat. The two looked at one another. My hands felt clammy, and my stomach churned with nervousness. Not that I'd ever admit or show that I was nervous. I just hoped that they would be understanding of my answer, much like Michelle had been when I'd told her.

"And what do you expect from working with Crystal Publishing?"

I gave them a smile. "An opportunity to work for

you and showcase my skillset and work ethic. I can promise you, you won't be disappointed. I'll work harder than anyone else and be more appreciative than you know. As requested, I sent you through the growth figures and campaigns I've been a part of and accomplished in the last twelve months while working at *Be True*. And I know I can do the same for Crystal Publishing."

The two looked satisfied by my answer. "Well thank you, Miss Bryer, for joining us today and we'll make sure to be in touch to let you know the outcome of the position."

"Thank you." I waited for the screen to go blank until I grabbed my bottle of water. *Damn it was hot in here.* It was after office hours and most of the staff had left by now. I packed up my laptop and bag and reached for my cell. There was a message from Alex and two missed calls from my mother.

Her number began calling again.

What was this, the tenth call this week? *What if something's happened?* A small part of me wavered.

"It's not my problem anymore," I said to myself quietly. And yet, I found myself answering the call.

"Sotiny! I've been calling all week and you haven't answered!"

I gritted my teeth. "Hi, Mom. I'm good thank you. How are you?"

"Don't be smart with me."

"I wouldn't dream of it... how could you possibly keep up then?" I spited.

There was a silence. "I don't know where I went wrong raising you."

I choked on my vile responses.

"I was calling to see if you'd like to come for Christmas."

Rage boiled my blood. "You can't be serious?" Never in a million years would I step into that house again.

"I thought you'd say that." She harrumphed, not sounding displeased in the slightest.

"Well, I was calling to remind you that your payment hasn't been going through lately. I've been barely living off scraps no thanks to you."

My nails dug into the edge of my desk. "I told you I was only sending you that money to help with chemo. And from what I'd heard your chemo finished a year before I stopped sending the money but you seemed to have neglected to inform me about that," I hissed. How many jobs had I worked to keep her afloat? How many years had I wasted on the very woman who'd hated me for the entirety of my existence?

"Your brother would be ashamed of you. He would've supported this household."

"Haven't found someone else's husband to mooch off yet, or has your waistline gotten too wide?"

She choked, taken aback. I pursed my lips, the acid dropping on my tongue. Nothing would've hurt my mother as deeply as to comment on her vanity.

"You're such an ungrateful ugly child. If I die frozen in this house because *you* couldn't support your own mother then—"

"Why don't you try getting a job yourself for once?"

"Why should I get a job?" She scoffed. "You know what, I don't know why I expected more from you. Such a cold unattractive heart. Disgusting. No wonder you're going to die alone."

I bit my lip. "Ditto," I breathed out, hitting the end button. Some things needed to stay in the past. And that was one box I'd vowed never to open again, time and time again.

Chapter 29

Sotiny
Age 16

"**M**om stop yelling at her!" Tyson screamed.

I stared out the window, a consistent throb and sting on my arm from where the broken plate had cut me. I tried to block their argument out. I wanted to be nothing more than a silent shell unseen. Seven. I'd now seen seven red cars on the road since leaving our place.

Tyson was driving with my mother in the passenger seat. They'd been arguing the whole drive. "What are the neighbors going to think now that she's caused a scene. It's all her fault!"

"Why were you throwing plates at her? You can't do that! You need to stop being like this!" Tyson yelled.

My mother seemed taken aback. Tyson very rarely raised his voice at her. "Everything I've done has been for you," she said quietly. "I do my best. Do you know how lonely it is being a single mother and giving everything I can to you children?"

Tyson scoffed. "Lonely? You invite every man who will look at you twice into our home. What part of that is lonely?"

She seemed abashed, her mouth agape. They'd never fought like this before. Then again, she'd never actually hurt me. Did I really mean so little to her? Retreating back into my shell, I heard the distant reply. *I meant nothing to her. I was only a burden.*

"I'm just trying to secure a roof over your head and offer you a better life and if it wasn't for this little wench here, I would've built a better future for *you*."

"Do you not realize you have two children? I don't need your money and support. Sotiny's the one who studies. Sotiny's the one who has a future. Why don't you see her?" he screamed, infuriated. It was the same boiling rage he'd directed at Alex with when they fought on the lawn. My mind drifted to Alex. I'd never seen him so angry. I'd never seen someone *care* so much for what happened to me. Tyson cared but this felt different. I began biting at my thumbnail, the red raw skin showing.

She scoffed. "The day after I gave birth to her your father left me because I had a *girl*. Do you know how heavily that's weighed on me since? All because of her I haven't been able to afford you the life you deserved."

"Are you sure he didn't leave because of how damn demanding and maddening you are?" She flinched under his words.

"Even you're turning against me now because of her. I wished I'd been able to swap her at the hospital," she said bitterly. And every fiber of her meant it.

Eight red cars. The car jolted beneath us, the old wagon hitting a hole in the road. The old car was barely able to stay on the road for weeks at a time but hopefully it would get us to the hospital so I wouldn't be stranded with them arguing.

I focused on the sting of the cut, almost savoring it. This is what I deserved. Maybe if it wasn't for me, Tyson would've had a better future. Maybe both Mom and him would have.

"That's it! The moment we're back, we're packing our stuff and leaving," Tyson promised. My eyes widened as he turned around. We could leave? He was choosing to take me away and leave Mom behind? "Do you hear me, Sots? We're getting out of here and—"

"Tyson!" I screamed as a red truck smashed into the front of the car, hitting his side. My head hit the glass window as everything around us spun, and I slowly faded into a bleak lonely darkness. And somewhere in there, I hoped I'd never wake up.

Chapter 30

Sotiny

I'd spaced off into the distance in my apartment building elevator. So much from the past felt like it was dragging itself up and rearing its ugly head. The audacity of that woman to call me and ask for more money! I bit at my thumbnail. Fake nails had been my saving grace, if it weren't for those, I'd be down to quicks again.

I searched for my keys in my handbag, slowing my pace down when I looked up. At the end of the hallway, amongst the peeling walls, Alex sat against the door, scrolling through his phone. His workout bag was beside him and he looked sweaty.

"What are you doing here?" I asked, falling short of my door.

He looked up, roughing up his dark-blonde hair. "I messaged you."

"That doesn't answer my question."

"On a scale of one to ten, how much would you be disgusted if I said I missed you?"

"Eight."

He smirked. "Okay what if I changed the question to how mad would you be if I told you I wanted to come and satisfy that sweet little pussy of yours?"

I considered it, keeping an icy gaze locked on him. "Four."

"And how mad would you be if I stopped by a bakery and bought two pieces of pecan pie as a bargaining tool?"

I rolled my tongue in my mouth. "Did the sweets touch your gross gym bag?"

He lifted a brown bag on his other side.

"I'll allow it. You stink." I pretended to kick him out of the doorway.

When he stood up, he pressed a kiss to my cheek, keeping his stinky distance.

"Well, I figured I could shower here."

"What's wrong with your shower?" I said, finally opening the door to my small apartment. I dumped my bags onto the counter.

"You're not in it," he growled. A chill ran up my

spine, the thought of being pressed up against the shower with Alex heated my core.

"Wow it's so messy already." He whistled in amazement.

"Shut up, I didn't know you were coming around," I said, self-consciously moving around carefully orchestrated piles. "And I know where everything is this way."

I grabbed a few of the comic books and filed them away, alongside the bag of novels, I'd bought only yesterday at the bookstore.

"Do you even have enough shelving to fit all these books?" he wondered.

"Shower, now." I pushed him toward my bedroom and the en suite. When he wasn't looking, I quickly sniffed the first towel on top of one of my baskets. I was certain this was the clean lot. As fate would have it, it was. I threw it in his direction.

He dumped his gym bag and phone on the end of my bed. I began folding the clean basket, my gaze drawing to him as he peeled off his sweaty shirt. The ripple of abs and strained muscle in his arms heated everything in my lower abdomen. Everything about him seemed bigger and more defined after he'd just worked out.

"For someone who was so begrudging of my

intrusion, you seem awfully quiet with your complaints now," he commented with an arrogant smile.

I looked away, focusing on my task at hand again, not giving him the satisfaction. Though when he turned his back to me, I sneaked another peek. Mother of all creation, how could someone's back be that muscular?

"I can feel your gaze, Sots," he called out. Shamefully, I focused on my laundry again.

"Presumptuous," I called out.

His cell began vibrating, curiously, I peeked. "Alex, you're mom's calling."

He leaned out of the shower, looking through the en suite door. He was lathering himself with shower gel. I was transfixed watching him as he rubbed over himself, almost wishing it was my hands rubbing down his stomach instead. "Can you answer it for me?"

"What? I'm not answering your phone."

"Relax she knows who you are and besides what if it's really important?"

"If it's really important you'll get your ass out here now and pick it up."

"Answer the phone, Sots," he called out.

A small growl crept out as I hit answer before I could break into a downward spiral of thoughts.

"Hello?" I answered. "Alex's phone." Shit of course she knew it was Alex's phone.

"Oh," his mother said on the other side. "I'm sorry who is this?"

I took a slow exhale, throwing a fiery gaze in Alex's direction. That cocky little dimple formed with his victorious smile.

"Hi, Mrs. Fields, I don't know if you remember me but it's Sotiny."

"Sotiny," she repeated. "The girl from next door? Well of course I remember you. I didn't realize you and Alex kept in touch?"

I bit at my bottom lip. "Yea I recently moved to New York and we bumped into one another."

Alex frowned giving me a disapproving glare. I threw my hands up in the air. What did he expect me to say?

"Wow that's incredible, how are you finding the city life?" she asked.

"Oh you know, it's a lot to take in," I said, eyeing her son from head to toe. "But I'm starting to enjoy it now."

"I always found Manhattan a little too busy for

my liking," she agreed. There was a silence. "Is Alex there?" she prompted.

Now with a towel wrapped around his hips, Alex plucked the cell out of my hand. "Hi, Mom."

I could hear her reply as I continued folding the clothes cross-footed on the side of my bed. He lay behind me, sprawled out on my bed as he rubbed his hand back and forth over my inner thigh. I could still overhear their conversation.

"I didn't know you and Sotiny had re-connected. Why didn't you say anything?"

"What were you calling about?" he laughed, completely avoiding her question.

"Well, you've ignored mine and your father's text and I was wondering if you'll be able to make it for Thanksgiving. Your brother and the kids are coming. I hope you don't skip another year."

"I know, sorry, I've been focused on a project at work that's been taking up some time." His hands trailed over my stomach and between my breasts, blazing a trail down my skin.

"Why don't you invite Sotiny as well? I'm sure it'd be nice to see her again."

I stilled under Alex's touch. The thought of going back to that town—right next door to where my mother lived—enveloped me in a coldness and rage I never wanted to admit. Sensing my discomfort, he quickly said, "Hey, Mom, I have to go but I promise I'll get back to you by tomorrow, okay?"

"As long as you mean it," she scorned.

"I mean it, Mom. I'll talk to you later." He hung up the phone.

"Sorry did you find that weird? My mother always thought you were a sweet girl and she loves hosting Thanksgiving so..."

"I'm not bothered by your mother inviting me to Thanksgiving, Alex."

He seemed confused as he sat up and wrapped his arms around me. It was a different kind of comfort. One I'd never known before. A touch I never thought I was worthy of. And something I didn't entirely trust that could last forever. I didn't really know anyone who had a long term relationship or how that looked. But I at least wanted to try with him earnestly. After so many years keeping everything shut so tightly, it wasn't easy.

"I don't ever want to go back to that town. I don't ever want to risk the chance of seeing my mother ever again."

"That's fair enough," he said, brushing a small kiss along the arch of my neck. I caved into it, realizing it offered me a gentle calmness. "What happened between you two?"

I stiffened. How much to reveal, lies and truth. I hadn't shared it with anyone, guilty and disappointed that I ended up helping her financially when she had cancer. I hated her more than anything, and yet after losing my brother, I couldn't quiet say no to helping her, scared I'd lose the only attachment to what family looked like for me. Would he be mad if he found out I wasted six years of my life running multiple odd jobs so I could have the cash to support her? I barely kept myself afloat during that time. Wouldn't he think less of me for not using my degrees in earnest? Or stupid for showing her any resemblance of kindness?

"As soon as I was accepted into college, I left only a year after you and I never looked back. And I will never go back to see her."

"I wouldn't expect you to," he said, pressing another kiss to my shoulder. I was acutely aware of the steam that rolled off him.

I turned to him, my gaze glued to his abs before rolling up, peeking through thick eyelashes. "Make me forget about it."

With his example many times before, I slowly grabbed his throat, my nails digging in. His gaze never left mine as they glossed over with that primal need I'd become so accustomed and aroused by. For one month he was mine. So, I would use everything he taught me and be fucked senseless in the process. I delicately trailed my fingers upward and slowly curled my nails into his cheeks, possessively holding him into place. I *liked* this feeling of having him at my mercy, just in the same way that he had me so many times before.

"Do you have those toys?" he huskily asked and leaned in to give me a kiss. I pushed him back before his lips could touch mine, enjoying the sense of control. I flicked my gaze from his perfectly rounded lips to those eyes, going into a frenzy remembering what his touch did to me.

"I do."

His throat bobbled at the thought. "You best remove those fingers, baby girl, before I bite them off."

I could see the hard press of his cock through the towel already. My mouth watered. We'd been fucking like rabbits ever since that first night and now I couldn't get enough of him. I was at his mercy as much as he was mine. Whatever this was between us, it was an unquenchable thirst.

I nibbled my bottom lip, a hot and bothered

fluster running through me as I leant down to kiss him. I melted into him. Lips, tongue, hands, legs and clothes being thrown about the place until I was beneath him. Without a second thought, he edged into me, his slick veiny cock spreading me apart to fill me whole.

I gasped, the sudden pounding stretching me into a position where I couldn't do much more than take it. "Which drawer are your toys in, baby girl?" he asked as he twisted and positioned me on top, so my back was to his chest. "Fuck." I could feel him so deeply inside of me, sitting on top of thick thighs. I found a rhythmic beat bouncing on his cock as I held myself upright on his thighs. How could something feel so good?

Cautiously, his thumb played around with my asshole. Oh fuck. Slowly, he pressed it in, my asshole stretching around him. I gasped surprised, thrilled and delighted. I kept bouncing. Couldn't stop bouncing as I gave way to his guttural demands and sweet whispers.

"More," I whispered. "I need more." Anal play was nothing new to me. I might've been a virgin up until two weeks ago, but it didn't mean I hadn't experimented on myself.

I flung open my side drawer, a delightful array of toys displaying themselves.

"You *are* devious," Alex murmured. He grabbed the silver rabbit, pleased by its size.

"I want your cum running down my legs," he soothed, squirting lube all over the rabbit. "I want you to scream out my fucking name." He yanked back my hair, looking down on me. "Do you hear me, baby girl? Only my name." I felt the cool tip of the lubed vibrator slip into my ass. A painful but pleasurable thrill passed through me. He watched my face as I squirmed under every inch going in. He grunted as he watched it, just as turned on and when it was fully in, with a small click, the vibrating began.

"Oh God!" I screamed, startled by its intensity.

"Fuck me, you're beautiful," he growled, slowly sitting me back onto his lap. With wobbly legs I hovered over him, slowly easing myself over him, entirely confused by all the sensations that were going on around me.

I held onto his shoulders like I was holding onto dear life. His cock filled my pussy so sweetly that I didn't know if there was a beginning or end. But as soon as I ever so slowly started rocking my hips, I cried out in sweet pleasure. How was I supposed to last when I was already coming undone?

Every bounce was like a tidal wave of pleasure rolling over me. I was so completely full. Alex's bruising kisses were everywhere, all at once. His careful hands and strength supporting me like a pillar. I threw back my head, riding him like I was possessed.

"Fuck me, Alex." I could feel myself dripping, unashamedly soaking through. I looked into his eyes, his own barely focused. With a smooth click the vibrator rolled over to the next level and I came undone. "Fuck me. Alex!" I screamed as everything released. I squirted all over him his thighs turning slick as I breathed out his name.

"Fuck, baby girl."

"I want you to come on me, please," I all but begged. I wanted him to be mine, just as I was his. He pulled out and I palmed his cock, feverishly pulling on him, demanding that he was as satisfied as me.

That tight muscle in his neck strained before he buckled into my palm. He came all over my stomach. A satisfied breath escaped me. I bit my bottom lip, as he continued to spill on me. Claw marks etched into his entire body. *Mine.*

"I think the whole neighbors heard me," I blushed, realizing how undone I'd become.

"Good," he said, nipping at my bottom lip.

Alex was everything my world never had. A raw wild edge to it. Never predictable and all the pleasures I'd never known. And I was frightful to think that I'd soon be without.

It was wild. Delicious. And entirely us.

"Looks like you might have to clean those clothes again though," Alex laughed pointing to the basket I'd started folding.

"I'm going to have clean this whole fucking room."

"Try house, baby girl, because I'm not done with you yet."

Chapter 31

Alex

Her house. My house. We'd become inseparable. After work. Before work. And how my cock throbbed for her even when we were apart.

We were in a staff meeting as she presented on behalf of Michelle—who still hadn't come back to work. And I knew exactly what lay beneath that hot gray pantsuit of hers. Purchasing lingerie had become my new personal hobby. It all looked good on her. And I especially enjoyed the photos she'd sent through. For someone who didn't like texting, she'd come around to the idea of sending a lot of content with few words.

I shifted uncomfortably, focusing again on the meeting. I could sense Damon's attentive gaze on me as I took notes. A few other people addressed the group, then everyone began their day. Sotiny and I turned away from each other, still pretending like we hardly spoke at all.

Damon called me into his office, like he did after most meetings. I closed the door behind me.

"What's going on?" Damon asked.

"With?" I asked, getting comfortable in the chair across from him.

"You seem different lately. And you've been skipping out on some of our gym sessions," he pointed out as he leant back in his seat.

"Are you missing me?" I pouted.

"I see enough of you here, one might think that's bad enough as it is."

I chuckled.

"You seem, I don't know... less wound up?"

"Wound up?" I laughed. I don't think anyone had ever described me as "wound up."

"Are you seeing someone? I've never seen you like this and it's weirding me out."

"Ironic coming from you, who was a complete space cadet only months ago when you started seeing Clover."

"I wasn't a space cadet," he mumbled.

"Nah just a lovestruck puppy."

He tsked.

"And no, I'm not seeing anyone. I'm just *really happy* to be at work."

"Mmm yea that must be it," he said, not at all believing me. "Well, besides that then, congratulations on your new contract. I still don't know how you were able to get them on board but I'm grateful for the sponsorship."

"No problemo. I'm not just a pretty face—you did hire me for a reason remember," I joked as I began walking out the door.

"Mmmm I'm still trying to remember that reason."

I closed the door behind me. As much as Damon and I discussed personal matters, this one I wasn't letting slip, especially because Sotiny and I decided to keep it our little secret.

I received another text. The moment I saw the picture, my cock throbbed. What was this girl doing to me?

She sat posed in her office chair, her buttoned blouse coming slightly undone revealing the red undergarment she wore beneath. It was the new one I'd had sent to her office only this morning. She'd already changed. In her hand she held the little white polished device I'd also ordered and added to the box. A nice little vibrating butt plug for my little vixen.

She casually smelt the gold sprayed rose in the picture as if all the other things weren't on display. What was this woman doing to me?

I beelined for her office, grabbing a few notes off the printer on my way so I looked like I had purpose waltzing into her office in the first place. I supposed it wasn't that abnormal, considering we were working on the same project. And there was only so much she could wind me up thinking that I wasn't going to react. I was a man with needs, after all.

I knocked on her door before letting myself in and closing it behind me. She didn't seem surprised by my arrival but squinted at me. "Rule number one," she began.

"No one at the office can know," I replied as I strode up and kissed her like I wish we were fucking instead. She moaned into my mouth. Every part of me wanted to rip those clothes off and bend her over this desk.

Another knock on her door. She pushed me away and sat back in her chair. I turned away pretending to assess the calendar on her wall, in a way that no one could see my semi-hard bulge in my pants.

"If we scheduled it for the Friday," I began.

"Yea I think that could work." Sotiny was the face of calm as Clover walked in.

"Oh, hey you two, sorry I didn't realize you were in here too, Alex." She looked between us peculiarly.

"We're just seeing what date we can schedule a meeting with Hayden to discuss a few things." Sotiny and I nodded in agreement.

"As I said, you can email it to me," Sotiny gritted out.

"I'll do that but let me know soon so I know if I have to shift a few things around. I'll leave you two to it."

"I'll try to get to it today," she agreed.

"I thought you were on a trip, Cloves?" I asked as I was leaving the room.

"Not until tomorrow but make sure Damon doesn't get into any strife while I'm away."

I chuckled. "I think the only strife he'll be able to manage is choosing the wrong tuna for your fat cat. That boy is homebound when you're gone."

"Don't let him hear that," Clover laughed.

"I wouldn't dream of it." I closed the door, following it up with a slow whistle. That was close and I'm no doubt going to cop an earful from Sotiny for it. I pulled the two tickets out of my jacket pocket. I also didn't have the chance to ask her about these.

Simon was searching around the printer. I handed him the few copies I'd grabbed. "Hey, man, I think I accidently grabbed yours instead of mine."

"Oh thanks. I was wondering where they went. Wait don't you have your own printer in your office?" he asked.

Right. "Yea but I thought it was broken this morning. So weird, right?"

Simon nodded with his happy-go-lucky smile. "That is weird but lucky it got sorted out."

I rubbed my jaw as I walked away unable to stop the arrogant smile on my face. Oh yea, Sots was going to be mad as hell, but damn it was worth it. And that fury was only going to be a turn-on.

Chapter 32

Alex

I received another cryptic text message and photo in lingerie captioned "come find me."

Considering it was the Sunday before the week of Thanksgiving, I deduced three libraries she'd be holed up in. Because at this time of year, she always restarted reading the *Harry Potter* series in a local library. She always went early so she could hire out the study rooms or capsules to have the entire room to herself and I doubted that much changed when it came to Sotiny Bryer's personal traditions and quirks.

With a bouquet of flowers in hand, I readjusted my leather jacket. I'd never done this for anyone. But we were on even ground now. We were really giving this a go, and I wanted to prove to her I could be the man I'd vowed to be. And in truth, I'd wanted to be this for her but was too much of a coward back then to back it up. I wasn't going to fuck it up twice.

I climbed up the few stairs to the local library, following the signs to the main desk. There were so many rooms and I was becoming confused. This, after all, wasn't my local hang out spot.

"Are you lost?" a young librarian with the name badge Tim asked.

"Ah yea, is it that obvious?"

He didn't reply.

"Can you tell me where the private study rooms are?"

The guy stared at me for longer. Was I really so out of place here? He pointed over my shoulder. "Down the hallway to the left."

"Thanks, Tim."

"That's Timothy to you," he said as he crossed his arms and narrowed his gaze.

Right.

The study hall was overshadowed by ceiling-high bookshelves. Each room was labelled by the participants who'd hired them out and for how long. Finally, on the fourth one down, I spotted Sotiny's name.

I tapped on it lightly. "Sorry this room's already

occupied." I knocked again.

"Sorry this room—" She slid the door open. "Alex?"

"Hey, baby girl." I pushed her back into the room.

"How'd you find me?" she asked. It was a small room with thin walls, and a white table with four chairs on either side.

"The Sunday before Thanksgiving you always find a library to start rereading this don't you," I asked picking up *Harry Potter and the Philosopher's Stone.* "You read the entire series every year. At least that was what I was betting on, lucky for me some things never change."

She seemed genuinely shocked that I'd found her. "Sounds kind of stalkerish."

"Some might call it attentive," I charmed and handed her the flowers. "There's something in there for you."

Delicately, she pulled the keychain out. "Really?" She bit her bottom lip, assessing the lego Hermonie Granger keychain. "When are you going to give up on that old nickname?" she asked with a coy smile, playing with the edges of my leather jacket.

"When you stop acting like a Goody Two-shoes."

"I thought you called me naughty the other night?"

Damn did this woman know what she was doing to me. I can't even remember the days before I was chasing her around in New York. How boring had the nights been before she came back into my life?

She pulled out the two tickets barely hidden amongst the bouquet of gold sprayed roses. She read them, a confused smile tugging at her lips. *Shit, was it a bad idea?*

"Two tickets to what appears to be a nerd festival over in Boston?" she curiously inquired.

I shrugged. "I mean if you're not into it we don't have to go but I thought we could spend the weekend there too. And some people dress up. And they sell heaps of those comic books that you like and stuff and I don't know was it a bad idea?"

"Alex Fields, are you trying to seduce me with comic books?" she purred, pulling my jacket in toward her and planting a kiss on me. "I've never done one of these. But I'm sure if you're with me I can brave the crowd."

That devilishly wicked smirk did all kinds of things to me. "Did you wear the lingerie I told you to put on?" I asked taking a step and pinning her against the door.

"Alex..." she whispered, losing her train of thought.

"Did you wear the lingerie I bought you like a good girl?" I trailed my finger down her jaw and neck, pushing aside the collar of the shirt ever so slightly to see the almond-colored strap.

Her breath hitched. "Alex, we can't here," she said in a quiet voice.

"Good girl." I crashed my lips against hers, fisting her hair. Her tongue was quick fire against mine. Despite her protests, she greedily pulled me into her.

"I want you bent over this table," I hissed into her mouth. She bit my bottom lip, that possessive expression flaring her lightening blue eyes. I nibbled at her jaw as she arched into me and began fiddling for my belt. I bit down hard on her throat, claiming what was mine. A small moan escaped her and I tightened my grip around her throat.

"You have to stay quiet, baby girl or we're going to get kicked out." Her hand wrapped around my cock and squeezed. A rasp escaped me and a satisfied gleam sparkled in her eyes as if she made her point.

"I don't know if I'm ready to show you this

lingerie. You see, it would appear I'm a Goody Two-shoes," she toyed, stroking my shaft. She played with it as if it were dough, moulding it tightly in her palm, ready to squeeze every ounce it had to offer.

"I want to push those panties to the side so I can fuck that sweet little pussy of yours. Didn't anyone tell you to be grateful for your gifts?" I pulled back her hair, arching her throat toward me. She squeezed hard again and another hiss escaped me.

"You want to fuck me hard, Alex?" she asked, releasing my cock. "And bent over this table." She tapped the end of the table and slid her knitted skirt up, revealing those creamy thighs. "So you can fuck my pussy?"

"I want your pussy dripping all over my cock," I growled in response. I thirsted for her filthy words, her pussy and everything that ensued. I was completely at her mercy.

"Then on your knees and eat me out first, the way I know you like," she commanded. At her command, I dropped to my knees, spreading open her thighs and admiring the almond silk I'd bought for her. "I have good taste," I commented.

"Yes, you do," she said, weaving her fingers through my hair as she hitched herself up to sit. I pulled the underwear down to her leather boots and buried my face into her sweet pussy.

She arched back, her hips motioning into me as she began fucking my tongue. "Alex," she whispered. "Fuck."

I bit her inner thigh, a small yelp coming from her. I cocked a smile, satisfied as I said, "You have to be quiet, baby girl, you don't want to be punished, do you?"

"And who will punish me?" she crooned, tipping her nail under my chin and raising me.

I stood up, rounding my shoulders as I pulled down my pants. "Are you sure you can stay quiet?"

"Are you so sure you can satisfy me?" She arched a playful eyebrow.

"Roll onto your stomach and bend over so I can see your ass."

With a smirk she did as she was told. Like the good girl she was.

I rubbed my cock against her wet pussy.

"You can try your hardest to make me scream your name. But I don't know... I'm a good girl you see."

I drove my cock into her tight pussy, the immediate hiss from her rewarding as she curved back toward me. I felt her loosen around me, that delightful flesh accommodating my size. This thing between us had taken on a life of its own. I couldn't not be with Sotiny Bryer. A thought that more often than not vexed me every night.

Chapter 33

Alex

Six years ago – Vegas

Vegas was the last place I expected to see Sotiny Bryer. We'd messaged one another over social media through the years but it was sheer chance that I saw a fellow college graduate tag her in a post stating they'd be celebrating their graduation here. As chance would have it, I was here on a work conference with Damon and friend Michael.

She'd finally graduated her dual master's degree in business and literary writing. I couldn't have been any prouder. It'd been six years since the accident with Tyson. And now I didn't know how to entirely face her. That guilt eating me alive for not being with her and fleeing out of shame after the argument we'd had just before the accident.

"Hello? Earth to Princess Alexis." Michael clicked his fingers in front of me. I was four whiskeys in and ever since I found out she was in the same city, I was looking everywhere for her. Every time I caught long strawberry blonde hair, my heart froze but it was never her.

I swatted Michael's hand away. "Sorry I'm just out of it today."

"Out of it, you're on a completely different planet. Can you properly celebrate the success we just had?" He wrapped his arms around Damon and me. "We need to celebrate. Let's hit this town any place, any strippers."

Damon grumbled his complaint. "You know I'm not a fan of the strip clubs."

"Party pooper," Michael hissed.

"Come on, Alex, what do you say?"

A short blonde bob caught my attention, wearing a short silver dress. My eyes were glued to her as she walked through the casino with two friends. *It couldn't have been.*

"Give me one second," I said shooting up from the table.

"I swear if you leave me with him for the whole night..." Damon grouched. He always complained but secretly enjoyed the escapades we took him on.

Sheepishly, I pretended not to obviously follow the group of three. *It couldn't be.* The woman in front of me was five foot nothing with black chunky boots that didn't do much for the dress but somehow offered edge to her style. They lined up, her friends cheering to purchase more gambling chips.

I towered over her, licking my lips. Her two friends noticed me first, their eyes raking over me. Her back was turned to me. Fuck, what if this wasn't her? What was I even doing?

The girl glanced over her shoulder, those striking blue eyes widening.

"Sots?" I said, barely audible.

"Alex?"

"Wow, oh shit, wow, it is you," I said, stepping back and really taking her in. She looked like so different with her hair, but it suited her. It was edgier but perfected. A simple gold necklace wrapped around her throat and those legs... I looked around. Who else had been checking out those legs?

"We'll catch up with you later, Sotiny, we'll be at the roulette okay. You look preoccupied," one of her friends said, gazing appreciatively over my build. Weakly, Sotiny waved them goodbye.

"Sorry, I didn't mean to disturb you and your

friends," I blurted, straightening my shirt self-consciously. *What did she think of me?* I'd never had any complaints from women but for the first time, I doubted myself. Did I still look like that teenager to her?

"They're not my friends," she corrected. Well good to see some things never changed. She never really did consider anyone her friend back then either. Why would she now? "They're just acquaintances I studied with. We're celebrating our graduation."

A suave smile crossed my lips. I already knew that. And I couldn't have been any prouder.

"What are you doing here?" she asked. "I didn't expect to see you here."

"I'm just here with some colleagues. I live in New York now."

"Wow that's pretty cool. It suits you."

We stood there in awkward silence. "Do you want another drink?" I asked noticing hers was empty.

"Umm, sure." She followed me to the closest bar. "I still can't believe you're here."

"It's a small world huh? So what's the big plan now? All graduated and stuff?"

She considered it for a moment. "Well for the time being I have an internship at a publishing house which looks promising."

"You know there's plenty of places in New York as well. I mean I could even ask around if you..." I trailed off. She was staring at me, a small smile creeping over her expression. "What?" I smiled back, unsure of what she found so amusing.

"You're still trying to take care of me. Even after all these years."

"Sir?" the bartender called.

"Oh umm can we please get two..." I looked down at her drink. "What was that?"

"Pina colada," Sotiny said.

"Yea and can we have two shots. Bartender's choice," I said with a wink. He smirked.

"Shots?" Sotiny inquired.

"Come on, Miss Granger, you've graduated, we've got to celebrate big, right?" And I needed something stiffer to push down whatever these nerves were. "Come on, it could be the biggest night of your life." I promised.

Hours later, after copious amounts of shots and pina coladas and whatever that other stuff was we drank, we wobbly stood in front of the fake Eiffel Tower. Considering how much time had passed, everything had changed and yet nothing at all. After the first drink, we both eased into conversation. The Sots that I knew—who had passion, a temperament and a *voice*—was still very much there.

"I'd love to go to Paris one day and see the real one," she said as she took another sip out of the plastic red bottle and straw hanging around her neck. "Shit I'm empty." She giggled.

"You've done that three times now." I grabbed her by the shoulder and pulled her in. I forgot how small she felt in my arms. "What if I take you one day?"

She scoffed. "When?"

With a cheeky smile, I toyed, "What about our honeymoon?"

A laugh erupted. That evil cackle of hers filling me with warmth. I'd always found it so contagious and rewarding when I could make her laugh. "Could you imagine it, Alex. You and me husband and wife? I'd destroy you."

"I think I could keep up."

"Really?" She hiccupped. Twisting to face me, she wrapped her arms around my waist, her height just reaching my chest. That delectable tensity rolled through us again. The raw and vulnerable feelings that engulfed me every day talking to and watching her from a distance as a teenager. All those childish emotions and lack of understandings rolled back through me—palpable tension.

But we weren't kids anymore.

Slowly, I dipped my head to hers, nudging my lips against hers for permission. Her breath hitched, a cautious pause, until she stood up on her tippy-toes to press into me. Our lips collided, a dance forming of its own accord.

I'd kissed many women, but none stood a chance against Sotiny Bryer. This delightfully wicked creature made untamed. Her kiss promised everything I wanted from her. That wild woman beneath the surface, promising delectable things in the way her tongue flicked against mine in a flurry.

She pulled away slowly, assessing me as if she'd seen me in a new light. "Would you really ever consider marrying a girl like me?"

Confusion ran through me. *A girl like her? Any fucking man would be lucky to have her.* "If you'd let me, I'd have you now."

"Then I'd say yes."

Chapter 34

Sotiny

I t'd been three weeks since we'd returned from Ithaca and so much felt like it'd changed. I didn't even recognize myself and so many others had commented too. From the staff at my local café, to my yoga studio. Is this what happiness truly looked like? Was it that transparent on people? Or as Alex had called it, did I finally have that stick removed out of my ass?

I sent the last email off to Michelle for the day. She was in the office for the day, holding up better than most other days but there was still some shiftiness around her response as to what the doctors had found and were saying. It worried me, and obviously Damon too, according to his expression as he checked up on his sister regularly.

Closing my laptop for the day, I noticed my cell buzzing with a call from an unrecognized Chicago number.

"Hello this is Sotiny Bryer," I answered.

"Good evening, Miss Bryer, it's Shantelle from Crystal Publishing. We had an interview about two weeks ago?" her singsong voice cooed through the phone.

"Yes, of course I remember," I said with a smile that I hoped she heard through the phone.

"We've come to a decision in our recruiting, and we'd like to offer you the position."

"Are you serious?" I asked. "Yes. Yes. Ahh," I stumbled. My heart was pounding. Yes. This was what I wanted wasn't it? I'd always worked so hard to get here, and yet now I wavered with hesitation. And I knew exactly why. Only one face came to mind.

"Amazing, I'll email you through the contract and you can look over it and let us know when you're starting date would be. We know you need to give notice at your current role, so the sooner you can let us know the better."

"Thank you," I said sincerely. "Thank you so much for this opportunity, you won't be disappointed."

The moment the call ended, I sat back in my

office chair, shocked. I wanted to scream and cry all at once. But instead, I stared at my desk. Shit, was I really moving to Chicago? Away from everyone? I narrowed down on that question. *Everyone?* It wasn't like I exactly made friends here. But it'd been the first place that had felt *homely* in a long time. And then there was Alex...

Michelle interrupted my thoughts by way of tapping on my door. "Hey, thank you for sending all that stuff through." She looked me up and down. "Are you okay?"

I tucked my hair behind my ear and held my hands together so I wouldn't chew at my thumbnail. "I got offered that position in Chicago."

"You did?" Michelle beamed. "That's great news! Well as great as it can be without me being disappointed that I'm going to lose my best assistant I've had in years," she laughed.

"But I don't want to leave you in this state when there's strain on your health and it really seems sudden doesn't it?" Was it just me or was it getting hot in here?

Michelle regarded me before saying, "Let's have a quick chat." She took a seat across from me. "What's really happening?" Michelle asked. "I've never seen you so... frazzled. When we had our first interview you told me blatantly, your end goal was to end up at a publishing house. I could see your drive and passion to get there. Why do you think I hired you for the job even though I knew you might pass through within a few years? So what's changed now?"

She brushed through her long black hair, crossing her legs. She was still the CEO but I also found I'd come to view her as a mentor of sorts, but could I count her as a friend? No, I didn't do friends. And Michelle had business relationships, not colleagues for friends.

"It is what I want. What I've always wanted," I clarified.

"So, what's the problem?"

"Things have just recently become complicated with someone I'm seeing here in Manhattan."

She seemed surprised. "I didn't know you were seeing someone. Ooh what's the gossip? If you give me a name I can do a check to make sure he's not married. You really have to watch some of them here in New York."

The irony that the man I was seeing was in fact married. And technically to me. "That isn't necessary."

"Well has it been a while that you've been dating?"

"Yes and no." I answered as best as I could. We'd technically been married for six years. And dating for three weeks. How would anyone make sense of that? How was I even meant to make sense of that? Taking in her confused expression, I elaborated. "It's complicated. I guess you could call it an on-again, off-again kind of thing."

"Okay. I can work with that," she said. "You know when Phillip and I started dating it wasn't exactly easy. I was a party girl always wanting to be social but maintain my family business and he'd just started his own accounting firm. We lived in different cities at times, and it wasn't easy. But we were always open in communication and honest with one another. If you find someone you want to make it work with then you do. And if it isn't meant to be then it'll fall apart on its own accord.

"But my biggest advice is that you have to do what makes your heart sing because the moment you hold yourself back from an opportunity for anyone you'll eventually resent them, in my opinion. It's only a decision you can make for yourself. Don't get me wrong, I'd love to have you here and that is still an option for you. I'm not exactly thrilled to send you off, but I respect you enough as a hard working woman to go for your dreams and I truly only want the best for you. So make sure you take the time to really consider what it is you want right now."

My chest squeezed at her words. "Thank you, Michelle, I really appreciate it."

"Any time and if you need to talk about these things or about Mr. Mystery Man let me know. I'm a bit disheartened though. If I'm being honest, I put a bet on against Damon that you and Alex were going to get together."

"What? Why?" I stammered. Did she know?

"Deplorable I know. And I shouldn't be admitting this to you as your boss, so don't sue me. But more or less think of it as a little laugh between two friends." *Friends.* "I don't know, you two always had so much riled tension between each other, I thought after all the fighting it might turn into something else. But I guess even I can be wrong. Sometimes. Rarely. But sometimes."

"No comment."

She laughed. "It's been nice to watch you slowly come out of your shell in the last twelve months, Sotiny. Know if Chicago doesn't realize how great you are, then there will always be a position and home for you here at *Be True*. But make sure no matter what you choose, it's what's best for you."

I'd always had a certainty about what was best for me. And for the first time in my life, that vision wavered. And I wasn't quite sure what to do with it. And even worse all these mixed emotions about Alex reminded me of how things ended last time, and I didn't want to hurt him again. Had we just been deluding ourselves with a fantasy again?

Chapter 35

Sotiny

Six years ago – Vegas

My heart pounded in my chest. Although I knew this was reckless, and a very logical part of me understood that even in my drunken state, I was also elated. I don't know how we got from the Eiffel Tower to a small wedding chapel with Elvis Presley officiating our ceremony, but everything in between didn't seem to matter either. I snorted, a fit of laughter wanting to break through at the guy impersonating Elvis.

Alex began chuckling; he was swaying just as much as I was. *This was such a bad idea.*

"I now pronounce you husband and wife." *Shit had we already given our vows?*

Alex grabbed the back of my neck pulling me in

for a kiss. The delicate taste of pineapple and licorice from a mixture of shots swirled in my mouth. His demand was needy, heavy and possessive. Every-thing about him felt so tense, almost like he was holding himself back. I pulled him by the edges of his shirt. *Mine. I don't care about anything else right now. Nothing else felt so right.*

"You're stuck with me now, baby girl."

Heat flooded my core. *Baby girl.*

"I could say the same to you," I said, smile beaming before another hiccup.

He chuckled, sweeping me off my feet and waltzing out of the chapel. With signed paperwork in one back pocket and two vending machine rings adorning our ring fingers, we were set for the rest of our lives. Well at least that's how intense Alex seemed right now.

I stared at the ring, squinting around the sun that had begun to come up. The ring looked as if it had diamonds in it, or perhaps that's just how I perceived it.

"Fuck, Alex, we just got married," I said out loud. He chuckled, his eyes hazy with liquor and lust. "Oh my God! What if neither of us remember this when we wake up?"

"We'll remember, most of it… probably."

"Stop, stop, let's take a picture." He gently put me down. "Here!" I grabbed his hand and dragged him in front of the Eiffel Tower.

"How the fuck did we end up back here?"

"Magic," I whispered.

He chuckled, pulling me in and kissing me again, his arms tightly wrapped around me like he would never let go. Everything else vanished around us. It was only me and him. And in so many ways, it'd only ever felt like us. A tiny sliver of pain crept through. No, there used to be someone else. *I wondered what Tyson might've thought. Would he have approved?*

Pushing away the uncomfortable feelings, I posed. "Let's take a picture, put your ring up and say cheese." We raised our hands with big cheesy grins. "Now we won't forget."

"I told you already, I won't forget," he said sincerely, pushing back part of my hair and cupping my face. "It's just you and me now, baby girl."

He meant it. I knew he did. It felt like whatever time had been wasted in the past had caught up to now. This foreign unsaid thing that had always been between us materialized into... marriage.

He flipped me over his shoulder and smacked my ass. "Now, I believe it's time we make this husband and wife thing official," he growled.

I tensed. A layer of ice running over me. *What if I was bad? What if he didn't like my body?*

In the matter of seconds, with waves of darkness and blotchy memory, we were in a hotel room and Alex was taking off his tie. It all seemed sudden. How did we even get to this hotel room? I mean it made sense to do this tonight didn't it?

"Sots, are you okay?"

Wow that alcohol was starting to sink in because my head was spinning.

"Yes," I lied, cupping his face desperately. I wanted this. I wanted Alex to see me. To approve of me. To *want* me.

I shoved him back onto the edge of the bed and ripped the corner of the condom packet with efficiency. Silently, I began clumsily unbuttoning his shirt. His hand rested over mine, pausing on the third button.

"What's wrong, baby girl?" he asked. I stared at the ring on his finger.

"It's nothing." I tried for the next button, but he stopped me. Another drunken hiccup escaped.

"Your hands are shaking."

"I just want you, is all," I said.

"Sots, why are you crying?" His hand reached up and swiped away the stray tear that spilled over my cheek. Surprised, I touched the place it had fallen. *Crying? Me?*

Baffled, I sat back in a chair and stared at him. "I don't know why I'm crying."

He knelt in front of me grabbing my hands.

"I just..." My bottom lip wavered. *Fuck what was this feeling?* "I just don't want to displease you, I think. I want to get it right."

"Get it right? Sots, there's nothing you could possibly do that would disappoint me."

I crinkled my fingers over his hand, unable to stop the shaking.

His eyes widened and he mouthed *oh*. "Sots, are you still a virgin?"

I sat there, head dangling, my mouth suddenly dry.

"We don't have to do this, Sotiny," he said, suddenly seeming to sober up. "Fuck I didn't know. I'm sorry."

"No, no, don't be sorry," I said, gulping at the evident bulge pressing against his pants. "I want this, Alex. I want *you*."

A low growl crept out of his throat. "Fuck," he said, standing up and walking in a circle contemplatively and brushing his hands through his hair.

"I'll do my best. You can do anything you want to me," I promised.

Suddenly he looked mad. "No. It's not meant to be like that, Sots. It's about what we both want and how we'll enjoy it."

Please don't make a big deal out of this. "No, it was going so well."

He rubbed over his face. "Fuck I'm too drunk to think this through right now. Let's just sleep on it and talk about it in the morning. I don't want you regretting anything tomorrow." His next step was definitely a wobble as he slid down the door, seemingly defeated and like he was fighting with himself all the same.

I tried so hard to focus on our conversation, as if every word passing was important.

"Please, Alex." I couldn't handle his rejection as well. That pent-up pain and rage from all those hard verbal slaps from my mother seemed insignificant compared to Alex's pullback right now. Please, anyone but him. Did he think I was hideous on the inside as well? Did he see through me?

"No, Sots, we'll discuss this tomorrow. I don't trust myself with you right now."

I curled into myself glumly. "Is it because I'm not like some of the other girls you've been with?"

"What? No!"

Another tear fell and my body shook uncontrollably. *Why'd I ruin it? I always ruined it.*

"Is it because you'll throw me away once you sleep with me?" My voice trembled. *I knew him and my brother had that stupid pact. One woman for only one night.* Another tear dropped at the thought of Tyson. Being near Alex *hurt.* Like some old Band-Aid being ripped off and the alcohol... it was making everything spin.

"No, I'm not just going to sleep with you and throw you to the side. Sotiny, you're the most beauti—"

"But that's what you say to all of them isn't it?" I said in a spiteful tone, my resolve stiffening. *I don't want to feel this. Whatever it is. I want it gone. I need Alex gone.*

"What?"

"You just parade around and sleep with whoever you want and then discard them. Like some male gigolo. It's disgusting. The receptionist, the cleaner, the bartender, anyone will do right? Except for me apparently? You're right this was a mistake, as soon as we wake up, we'll get an annulment. I can't believe we actually went through with it."

My words were like acid. A lethal expression

marred his beautiful face as he gritted out, "I'm not signing any damn papers and tonight wasn't a mistake. If all you think I'm good for is using my dick then I don't know how my small peanut-sized brain is going to comprehend signing a paper. I can't believe you! Are you serious right now? You're trying to push me away again! You're trying to run!"

"I'm not trying to do anything." I shrugged, wiping the final tear. Satisfaction swept through me as I collected my emotions and hid them away once again. I felt in control. "I'm just saying you're a one-hit wonder, right? That's what you two always laughed about wasn't it? I wonder what he'd say about us getting hitched."

Regret. I hated every word I spouted. I saw the immediate effect it had on him. Especially the mention of Tyson. But I needed him away and gone. This *feeling* hadn't been an issue for years and only now was it flaring up.

"I think you should leave." I felt suddenly sober, like a cold bucket of water had washed over me. And by the way he looked back at me, I could see it in his eyes as well. Although when he stood up, it was clumsy.

"I can't believe you're really doing this again."

"If memory serves correctly, I already told you

once I didn't want to leave with you. Not that you were around much after Tyson's death. So why would you think a second time would be any different?"

Cold. Hurtful. A direct bullet to the chest. My ugly words were reopening wounds that should best be left in the past. I felt like I was forcing my own to bleed in the process. But as soon as he was gone, it'd all be okay. *I would be okay.*

Fury and hurt crossed his expression as he pulled out the marriage papers. *Fuck. What had we done?*

"And we'll have to sort that out. We were dumb and—"

"I'm not signing jack shit," Alex seethed. "I meant what I said and I'll be fucked if I'm going to let any other man marry you. And I doubt anyone else would be willing to put up with your shit."

I felt the lump in my throat harden.

"You're just running away again." It sounded more of a plea, a question. An inquiry of redemption.

"Then doesn't that make one of us smart because you and me will always head towards a train wreck. Now get out."

"You're right about one thing, Sots," he said coldly. "Not reaching out to you had been the best decision of my life. I wonder if your brother would be proud to realize you turned out as cold as your mother." He slammed down the papers on the side table and stormed out. A weight set in my throat and heart. A combination of pure rage and fear sunk heavily into the pit of my stomach, all of my insecurity exposed. His words hit hard. She was the one person I tried to escape. The one person I never wanted to be like. And it had crossed my mind that maybe my indifferent, cold personality mirrored hers. But to hear that from Alex of all people... *What the fuck had I done?*

I picked up the nearest glass and threw it at the door, all these explosive emotions overtaking my actions. I screamed. That pure hot hatred for him overtaking anything I thought I'd felt for him before. Tears spilled over my cheeks as I considered how I'd so easily fallen for his trap. How I'd stripped myself open for something too good to be true. I wasn't a woman capable of some fairy-tail ending. Especially with the likes of someone like Alex Fields.

Chapter 36

Sotiny

"Hey you," Alex said, kissing me as he opened his door holding a spatula. A complicated aroma of herbs hit my nose.

"Is it safe to come in here?" I queried, letting my nose lead the way into the kitchen.

"You're very funny," he regarded, hanging my jacket on the hook. I side-glanced the loose sweatpants he wore, my gaze stopping on his bare chest. If he were to wear only that at a restaurant, I was certain he'd have a loyal clientele. Even if the food was inedible.

"I don't remember cooking being one of your strengths," I said, walking into the kitchen. "Remember that one time we tried to cook your mother's recipe for the vanilla cupcakes with butter-cream icing and we almost somehow set the house on fire?"

He chuckled, presenting a container full of buttercream frosted vanilla cupcakes. I eyed him. "You made this?"

"I might've learnt how to cook a few things," he commented, raising one of the cupcakes.

Tempted by my favorite sweet, I swiped a delicate finger full of the icing. I purposefully toyed with it in my mouth, allowing a small popping noise to squeeze out as I sucked it off. "So far so good."

He kissed the corner of my mouth. "So far I'd agree." His smile was contagious. "Oh shit." He dropped the container into my hands and raced for the oven.

The moment he opened the door, smoke billowed and he flicked a handtowel back and forth.

"What was that supposed to be?" I asked, plonking myself at the marble-tiled island bench and admiring the golden hanging ball features. I took a bite of the cupcake, pleasantly surprised that it wasn't too dry.

Alex sulked, staring at it in disbelief. "Roast beef and vegetables?"

I leaned over the counter, staring at the char-coaled heap. "Were you keeping an eye on it?"

"I mean... yea. Until I realized the time and then I wanted to get changed and ready before you came over."

"So you got distracted by your pretty self in the mirror, huh?" I asked, trying not to laugh. "Who's a pretty boy?"

"Don't do that," he teased, rolling up the tea towel into a thick rope. "Or I'll have to spank that little ass of yours."

I took a big bite of the cupcake, purposefully keeping my mouth closed. Surprisingly, it tasted the same as I recalled his mother's. "So what made you decide to cook all of a sudden?"

"I wanted to do something different for you. And I don't think I've cooked for a woman. Ever. So, if all went to plan it was supposed to woo you."

His endearment wasn't lost. A swelling formed in my chest. He was really trying at this. It also made me feel not so estranged to the idea of dating Alex. We were the same. Both foreign to this concept of dating and relationships. And instead of jabbing him for being a player, I found a more endearing and vulnerable side to him.

"You really haven't had a girlfriend?" I asked

skeptically. Surely someone had grabbed his attention for more than one night. He was a ridiculously attractive, successful, charismatic thirty-three-year-old man in Manhattan, surely someone had made an impression on him.

"Maybe I had one in grade school once," he contemplated, not so seriously. "You know this thing with us," he said carefully, watching me with every slow step he took toward me as if I were some frightful deer about to run. "It's new for me too, Sots. I've never done this with anyone. And I want to do it right this time."

I felt the heavy weight of the business proposal hanging over me like deadweight. I had to find the right time to tell him. But how could I tell him without hurting him or turning it into an argument? And how could I protect myself? I hadn't even processed the thought of this ending yet. Although I knew it wouldn't last forever, I'd hoped to have a little longer with him at least.

"I really want that too," I said truthfully, even with my doubts of how we'd be able to navigate it.

"But this I think I failed at." He pointed at the charcoaled meal. "Want to order in?"

"Or we could eat this entire container of cupcakes?" I suggested brightly.

A smile passed his lips as he walked over and placed his hands on either side of my stool. He kissed me sensually, not demanding like his usual bruising kisses. But sweetly, endearingly—lovingly even. I wondered if he was aware of our one-month trial coming to an end as well. He took a bite of my cupcake and sauntered off into the living room to grab glasses and a bottle of wine.

"So, I was curious," I shouted through the open frame into the living room. "You said that you had property elsewhere. Is that just to build a portfolio or do you have any interests moving there?"

Walking back in with two glasses of white, he thought for a moment. "I bought my first property I think two years out of college. And it's mostly just for my portfolio or if I even feel like an extended vacation. I like having real estate. But I don't think I'll ever move. New York has mostly everything I needed. Well up until a year ago and then it had everything I needed."

His gaze was penetrating, and I felt flustered under the heat. Wow he was laying it on thick tonight. But hadn't he always been transparent like this?

"I need to quickly wash my hands after all the icing, I'll be right back."

"Right, I'll order us some Chinese."

Tiptoeing into his en suite, I washed my hands and clamped my wet hands on my face. How was I going to tell him? What did I even want to say? Somehow I just didn't want to fuck this up but I knew in my heart of hearts it was broken from the very first day we'd agreed to give this a go, if even for a trial month.

Was I really willing to uproot my entire life over one month of great sex? But it was more than that, no matter how I tried to justify it logically. I fanned myself walking back and forth. Fuck.

I couldn't find a towel to dry my hands and opened the first draw. Nope. Second. Nope. Third. My eyes narrowed on the small chest hidden away. I quickly glanced outside the en suite door and downstairs. Alex was still ordering Chinese over the phone. Curiosity got the better of me. I opened it up, sucking in a harsh breath, knowing that what I was doing was wrong. I almost expected something to jump out and grab me for it.

Two things sat in the hidden box. Both telling me more about how Alex felt than he'd ever been able to say in words. The cheap ring from our wedding night in Vegas with a single printed photo of us drunkenly showing them off, childishly smiling.

And all I had to show for that night was the marriage certificate which was only intended for the divorce papers I'd demanded he signed six years later. I hung my head in shame. Fuck, how deep in this was I really?

"Sots? Did you want the deep-fried ice cream?" he called out from the living room. I snapped the little box shut and put it back on the bottom draw as if it burned my hands. "Never mind, of course you do."

He could only still have this for one reason, surely? Didn't that mean... that maybe this was real? Maybe Alex Fields did care about me in the same way I hated to admit I'd felt about him all that time ago.

I sat on the closed toilet lid, taking deep breaths and calling in that fortified wall and mask that often bolstered me into speaking logic and wit.

Steadily, I took the staircase, my heart in a flutter again when I watched him go about his business, half naked in the kitchen. Granted, it wasn't his strength, but it was still hot as hell.

I took my seat and downed half the glass. He was glumly scrapping the entire dish into the bin.

"Couldn't salvage any, huh?" I casually said.

He shook his head back and forth, his bottom lip thick. "I tried, I couldn't even cut through the meat."

I winced. After a long pause, I grew the courage to ask. "What happened that night between us in Vegas?"

It had been for the longest time my personal vendetta and focus of hatred. It seemed like a dream come true and then popped into a hard-slapped reality. And everything after that fell apart, it was only weeks later my mother reached out about her cancer. And the rest had become history. I'd fantasized about what I might've said to Alex Fields if I saw him again, all that hurt and pain that had been simmering for years. And yet after only twelve months of being in close proximity with him, here we were. Me in his bed for the last three weeks, contemplating whether I was willing to throw away the dream I'd longed to have in exchange for something with him. And he had no intention of moving anywhere else. It was preposterous. Outrageous. And yet heartbreaking to think of letting him go. He'd become, once again, my form of comfort and someone important in my life. Maybe even the only important person in my life.

He raised an eyebrow, a lazy unsure smile crossing his features. "I was wondering when we'd talk about this," he said, taking the stool across from me. He dragged mine closer to his, propping his legs on either side of mine and caging me in.

"I don't regret marrying you, if that's what you're asking?" he said, taking my hand and rubbing his thumb over my knuckles. "It's just that night there was a lot of alcohol involved. I didn't realize you were a virgin and... and..." He struggled to find the words.

"Say it, Alex." Every word he said mattered. Every belief he had would define our future, if we had any whatsoever.

His shoulders sagged. "I always promised your brother I'd never touch you. But I'd be lying if I didn't say I wasn't crazy about you before we made that promise. That day when your brother died." He hesitated. "I've never forgiven myself for the fight we had before. Or not going to his funeral afterward. What right did I have after all of that? And I held a lot of guilt around you. I avoided you and left only months later. I should've stayed and looked after you, but I ran."

"It wasn't your role to look after me, Alex."

"But it was. It was your brother's and then he was gone. And it might've been partly my fault. If we didn't have that fight—"

"Alex," I said, cupping his jaw. "It was never your fault."

A tear sprung to his eye. "Your brother was my best friend, I never thought after that stupid fight that he'd be in an accident. I would've never done or said those things if I could go back in time. I was careless and I was angry and then I'd abandoned you. And that was a hard reminder when we'd wound up in that hotel room in Vegas."

"No, no that's not right," I clarified, grabbing his hand. I'd never seen the cheerful and bashful Alex, look so broken. But his guilt I understood. That split moment Tyson looked at me as he was driving. Waking up with the realization that the only relative who ever cared for me had died immediately on impact. That he'd left me behind and my mother blamed me for his death. That still weighed heavily on me, even now. And I knew part of my thinking was obscure. But I couldn't help but believe all those lies I was fed because deep down, I did feel guilty. If only I'd spoken up. If only I'd stood against her. But even now, I was still too scared. Too embarrassed by how her words impacted me. But I could never voice it out loud. These voices and monsters I lay with every night weren't his to fight. His weren't the same as mine, but they were cut from the same cloth.

Manifested out of the same ugly torment of an accident and losing a loved one. And on so many occasions, I'd wished it had been me taken instead of Tyson.

Alex's voice wavered slightly. "That night when we'd married, it's like it all raced back to me that guilt and hurt. And then when you spoke about me being so easy with women, it hurt mostly because it was true but also because you couldn't see me as anything else. I wanted to always be there for you. I'd panicked and felt unworthy. And those things I said about you being like your mother... I was angry, Sots. I never meant any of it. You're the complete opposite to her, you're kind and loving."

I didn't realize after all this time how desperately I needed to hear him say those words, as relief washed over me. Because I felt the truth in his words. I'd said horrible things that night too. I wasn't naive enough to excuse him for saying them. But I couldn't deny my own responsibility in that argument either. "I'm sorry I pushed you away as well. I was scared and you were right, I ran away and I'm sorry for that. What I said was vicious and hurtful and all the painful things I've said up until now. You deserve someone better than me, Alex." My lip quivered. "That's the absolute truth."

"That's the biggest lie you've told yourself yet. I only want you, Sots. It's only ever been you."

My heart twisted with his sincerity. Behind the player was still that sweet teenage boy I'd first fallen for. And there was no way in hell that I could tell him I was about to leave him again. Not tonight

The only thing I could do was reciprocate his feelings in earnest. By saying the things I couldn't through words and dote on him with kisses and a love that I knew would haunt me for years to come. I'd give myself tonight. Us tonight. But by week's end, I'd be forced to bring our arrangement to an end and that made my kisses and need for him to fill me only more desperate. How could I choose to lose him again? How could I actively let him go? I was in the same light, pulling the trigger on myself in the process.

Chapter 37

Alex

I bounced back and forth, feigning left and right a little more enthusiastically than usual.

"What's gotten into you today? You seem 'more' lately, if that's even possible."

I clicked my tongue. "Tell me how you really feel, Damon?" I laughed.

"It's just I don't remember the last time you were so enthusiastic on a Monday morning. You're usually recovering from the weekend still slightly hungover."

I beat my gloves together. "It's not that bad and even when I do go out it's only a few drinks and wherever the night usually takes me. I'm not hungover every time," I said, swinging and stretching my shoulder.

"Is it possible you didn't go out this weekend?" He was staring at me skeptically.

"Would that be so bad?" I laughed.

"Okay, what's seriously happening with you? These last few weeks you've been so weird and I don't know if I should be concerned. Are you having a midlife crisis?"

I chuckled. "No, I'm not having a midlife crisis but if I were, you'd be the first I'd be dragging to Vegas or wherever the muse takes me when I do have one." I realized then maybe his concern was deeper than I gave it credit for. With Michelle's health all over the place, I wondered how much that strain was really holding over the Brogardt family. Often Sotiny would pull out her laptop late in the evening to follow up on emails and take majority of the work off Michelle's schedule.

"I'm fine. Just trying something new is all. And what about you? Any update with Michelle?"

Damon slumped against the edge of the boxing ring, taking a breather for some water. Terry, one of the owners—built like a body builder—walked past whistling. "You guys don't miss a day, huh?"

"Lately it would appear," Damon said, eyeing me.

Terry waltzed his bear-sized body in the direction of the weights.

Damon leant against the corner thoughtfully. "I kind of miss the days where the discussion mostly revolved around Cassidy's new dating flings and the highs and lows of her many adventures." He chuckled.

Ah, Clover's friend from her previous role at *Candice Magazine*. I'd partied with Cassidy a few times and she was a known serial dater but for good reasons. The girl was beautiful. "How is the bouncy chirpy blonde from *Candice Magazine*? I thought she was like some heiress or something so why is she slumming it with so many idiots?"

Damon arched an eyebrow and I feigned forgiveness. "Right, I forgot, Clover can't know she's an heiress because Cassidy doesn't want anyone to know." Kind of hard when the Brogardt family know most distinguished families. And besides, I felt like we were somewhat going off the point. "So now?"

"I'm stressed," Damon admitted. "Michelle's never been like this. And all I can think is what if it's cancer like what took Mom?"

"Shit, man," I said, pulling off my gloves. That was heavy. "I know it's hard not to think like that but I think by now they would've found something if it is. Everything will be okay. Michelle's like one of the healthiest people we know."

Damon gave me an effective glare.

"Okay she may have a borderline drinking problem but let's put that to the side." I cocked a smile. The woman loved a wine or two on any occasion. "What happened to your mother isn't going to happen to your sister. They've been checking for all of that already and no news is good news."

Damon nodded reluctantly. "Yea. I'm just worried about her and with the poor timing of Sotiny leaving as well, I have concerns for what stress it might add training a new assistant, especially in the days she can't come to the office."

My stomach dropped. A suddenly hard lump in my throat. *What did he just say?*

"Wait. What? Sotiny's leaving?"

"Yea she was offered a job in Chicago with a publishing house on Friday apparently. I spoke to Michelle last night about it. She doesn't have an exit date yet but I imagine it'll be around a month or something and then Michelle will try to push herself and I'm just worried about her is all."

I was stunned into silence.

"Alex?"

Everything became a blur. A twisted knot in my

stomach rose up before I shoved it back down. *She what?* We'd spent the last two fucking days together and she'd said nothing. And I'd said all that stuff, running my mouth about her brother and how I felt about us, and this is how she returned the favor?

"Earth to Alex?" Damon snapped. "What's with you lately, man?"

"Sorry, I just remembered something. Michelle will be okay, man, and we'll do whatever we have to make it as stress-free without her." I tapped him on the shoulder, dipping underneath the rope.

"Are you leaving already?" he shouted behind me. "I thought we were just having a break."

"I just remembered I forgot something, sorry. I'll make it up to you tomorrow," I yelled back, trying for nonchalant. My whole body was a funnel of pure red-hot rage and there was no way in hell I was taking it out on my boss in a ring. I'd laid everything open to her and she just sat there... knowing this whole time she was going to leave.

My blood absolutely boiled. What a wicked insensitive creature she was indeed. I hadn't realized this whole time I was just some fucking pastime for her.

Chapter 38

Sotiny

I took a mouthful of my coffee while flicking over the notes and deliberating the event we were hosting in less than a month's time, right before Christmas. In celebration and in grand announcement we'll be hosting a campaign in vain of Hayden Zilch onboarding and the magazine we'll be creating together.

I chewed at the end of my pen while deliberating the date. I had to give Crystal Publishing an answer by this week as to when my start date would be. I'd gone over my contract and although it was slightly less money than working here it had the potential to grow and offered bonuses as well. I'd looked at property in Chicago and for the most part there were plenty of options. It's not like I had any dependants, and I could always roommate with someone until I had the down payment for my own place.

I jumped out of my seat as Alex stormed into my office. "When were you going to tell me?" I caught my coffee in time, having almost knocked it over.

"What?" My heart raced.

"That you're moving to Chicago!"

I felt myself pale. Scanning through the door behind him, I couldn't see anyone, but it didn't mean that no one could walk in at any time. He was in a fluster, still wearing his workout gear. My head was whirling and a cold chill ran down me.

"Wha—"

"We spent all weekend together and you didn't think to mention it?"

My heart stopped. I stammered out, "I was trying to find the right time and I haven't decided on anything yet."

He threw his head back and laughed. "We spent all weekend together! How did you not find the time? Or did you enjoy watching me bleed out in honesty, so you could take more satisfaction in this little 'experiment' of yours."

"Satisfaction?" I hiccupped. He wasn't thinking clearly. His anger had gotten the better of him. And how that shattered my very existence to see him like this. Especially because of me. But nor would I cower under his wrath, letting him speak down to me like a child. "The reason why I didn't tell you *yet* was *because* of everything you'd said, Alex." I felt cold and flustered all at once. *No, this wasn't meant to go down like this.*

He scoffed. "So while it's okay for me to be honest, you don't feel like that applies to you? Isn't that a point of a relationship?" he sneered.

"What relationship?" I spat out, that automatic reflex to build a wall and protect myself by striking out. I was trying my hardest to be the face of calm. But didn't I already have my doubts that this would blow up one way or another. Wasn't this the third time now it was ending badly between us. We were like electrical cables, sparking and blowing up every time we saw one another. Maybe we were destined for the same rerun.

"You can't be serious?" he growled.

"So we had an agreement for one month and we haven't spoken about what 'it is' yet," I quoted in the air, ice dripping over every word. I couldn't fight his fire with fire. But neither did it feel right. Arguing like this. Not after everything we'd been through. Not after how right everything had been.

"You have got to be kidding me, after all this time

you honestly haven't changed one bit," he seethed. "As soon as it gets too hard you crawl back into your shell."

I restrained my jaw from dropping and clenched it instead. Fine, if that's how he wanted to play it. Then fine. "That's right I'm some insensitive shell. Always have been and always will."

"Don't put words into my mouth."

"Why? You certainly seem to think you know a lot about me. What I'm going to do. What I'm going to say. I mean you probably think I've already accepted the job, handed in my resignation and am off within the month, don't you?" I could feel the swell in my throat. Why was it always like this, why did we only fight with the words we knew would hurt one another the most? And even when I knew I was doing it and could see his hurt and only wanted to tend to him, the words blurted out effortlessly.

"Haven't you?" he said, abashed.

I remained silent.

"This is a joke. I don't know why I tried so hard. You drive me mad, woman. I don't know left from right with you anymore." He took a breath. "I told you I was in this. And I'm going to ask you one last time, where do you stand with us?"

I bit my bottom lip, so it wouldn't tremble. *I want*

you. I need you. I care for you. Fuck I think I'm in love with you. But could I step off that ledge into the unknown and tell him that? To allow myself to be broken into a million pieces like the last man that promised me pretty things. And this was different. Alex wasn't Tyson. Alex was here, living and breathing in front of me, pleading for an answer. And in return, all I could say was "I don't know." My voice broke as I held in the avalanche of emotions that wanted to flood over. "I still think you deserve more."

And that was my truth. I was a little broken thing. Emotions and joy, all the things he was, I struggled with day-to-day. We were completely different in every way. And where he might've enjoyed gambling with his emotions and vulnerability, I could not.

He stood there, mock-laughing and shaking his head. His rage was palpable and oozing from him. I never feared Alex's temperament and for the first time, I found myself too tired to really lift my own sword. I might've not been entirely vulnerable or open with him, But I'd let him have this final last strike. The moment he cut me out of his life, the better it'd be for both of us. And I was too much of a coward to be able to do it myself.

"Then I guess that's my answer," he said, throwing his hands up in disbelief.

A small low grunt startled us both. Standing not too far away from Alex was Michelle, arms folded over her chest. "Despite being surprised about this situation I think it's best you leave for the day, Alex. Before others start coming into work. I care for you like a brother but don't bring this shit into work," she reprimanded.

Hurt and offended, Alex offered one small begrudging nod and tightened jaw, then walked in the opposite direction. Defeated, I sat back down in my chair, waiting for the same reprimand. I focused on my breathing, mustering all the broken fragments to come back together in a twisted ball and push it back down into the place I never opened up again. I refused to cry. And yet, all I felt was sorrow. It was similar to the pain that twisted at my chest when I stood at my brother's funeral, realizing I'd been left behind and the same distinct impression that it was all my fault. That guttural plea that followed me for years, wishing it had been me instead of him.

Michelle leant against my doorframe, pointing in the direction Alex left. "The 'It's complicated' status?"

I avoided her gaze, smoothing over my bob.

"Yes," I squeaked out. It was barely audible. So I nodded instead. I tried to clear my throat. I had to get my shit together. This was for the best. This was what needed to happen. Wasn't it?

"Sotiny, how about you have a day off too. I'm feeling alright today, and you deserve it. Clear your head a little. Take a walk. Reflect on what you're doing and if it's the right thing for you."

"Is it the right thing?" I squeaked, feeling like a child in the way I looked up at her, searching for answers. Everything was twisted and fragmented. I couldn't remember what was right or wrong anymore.

"Only you can answer that. But what I can advise is you need to take the day off. You're an incredible woman and can have whatever you want, so don't fall short of having it all if that's what you want."

When she closed the door, I only found confusion in her stead, not entirely understanding what she was insinuating. My dream and goal, she was surely talking about that. To keep focused on my vision. But perhaps going for a walk was the right idea. Even if I tried to bury myself into work now, I'd only get carried away by the memories of Alex's angry and twisted expression.

I did the right thing didn't I? So why did I feel like balling up into an insignificant blob under my quilt, never to see the outside world again? This hollow feeling that remained, was foreign and more devastating than when he walked out on our wedding night. Because now I actually knew Alex Fields. And fuck me it hurt because I was certain I was already in love with him.

Chapter 39

Alex

The wind whistled, kicking up my jacket as I stood in front of Tyson's grave. I'd only ever seen it from the distance. I even watched the funeral hiding beside a tree like a coward where no one could see me. At the time, I felt like I didn't have the right to be here. I still wasn't sure if it was okay even now.

It was confronting to say the least, standing in front of this tombstone and the ghost that had haunted me for years—fifteen to be exact—since the accident. I placed the bouquet of flowers down knowing he'd probably hate it and give me shit for it but I didn't know what else to do in a situation like this. I sat on the withered wooden bench across from his grave and rested my arms on my knees as my head hung low. I stared at it, the size of the tombstone seeming to only grow.

Since I'd decided to come back home for Thanksgiving and for the first time, it felt right to visit Tyson. "I really fucked up," I murmured out loud. It had taken me too long to get here. And what did I have to show for all that time? A big blowout with his sister, the one woman I'd been sworn off. And I'd really fucked that up too.

I wondered what Tyson might've looked like now if he hadn't passed at seventeen. Whether he would've gotten Sotiny out as he'd promised when he turned eighteen. I wondered if he might've settled down and had children, or if together we would've continued our 'one night only' rule. I scoffed. It was his idea in the first place and yet maybe a small part of me deep down wanted to maintain that tradition, as if it was the only part of him that I could hold onto.

I wrangled my fingers. Well, there was something else he left me. Sotiny.

I'd always wanted to take care of her in his stead. I thought about her regularly, even when we weren't connected. Had it been simply out of obligation that I wanted to watch her grow and take care of her. I tried to change my way of thinking but that did nothing to the reality of knowing that deep down I fucking loved her. Every day in that office for those twelve months was like shackling my restraints from reaching out and touching her. In some way, I felt like I deserved her scrutinizing gaze and clipped tone because at least I provoked something out of her. I had hurt her and I deserved her scorn. But now it was different. I'd seen that sweet side of her. Loved it just as much as her sharp tongue.

"I'm sorry," I said out loud. How much would Tyson hate me for everything that I'd done? The fact that I ended up with his sister anyway, despite his warnings.

The wind howled again. "You know, despite how shitty the situation is. At least our argument somehow brought me to here," I said out loud as if I were talking to him. I probably sounded like a madman talking to himself if anyone overheard, and yet I found solace in it. "I'm sorry I didn't come sooner, man."

My throat locked up as I imagined exactly what Sotiny witnessed that day of the accident.

My mother was a nurse at the hospital on the day the crash had happened. When she'd returned home and broken the news, I also overheard her crying to my father that night. Recalling the moment Sotiny woke up and found out the news about Tyson, that her hallowing scream could be heard all the way down the hall for hours.

A tear pricked my eyes. I wanted to run to her side that day . But how could I after the fight we'd just had? The way she'd looked at me after, I was almost certain they'd hate me and her mother definitely would've shooed me away.

If it hadn't been for me, then maybe they wouldn't have been in that car on that day. But a more reasonable part of me realized onus was on their mother for hurting Sotiny in the first place. And it was an "accident." Tyson had run a red light, the only saving grace that everyone else involved was able to walk away. A lump formed in my throat at the thought of Sotiny not making it out.

"Maybe that's why I was too scared to say my goodbyes." Because I wasn't there to protect her and make it all okay. Because I hadn't been able to save Tyson. And all those horrible things I'd said and done right before he was taken away from us.

My knuckles and fingers were white. "I should've done more for you." But what could I have done? Nothing, just like the rest. It was out of everyone's control. I realized maybe that's why Sotiny clung to routine and control so much. I'm sure even she probably wasn't aware of some of her habits.

"But we're not kids anymore," I reasoned. For so long I let it hang over me like deadweight, what he might've thought about me coming back into Sotiny's life. Being an accomplice to getting her that job at *Be True* so I could see her again. If he had grown up with us, wouldn't he have changed as well? Maybe his opinion of us might've changed too?

A splatter of rain dropped on my shoulder and I looked up into the overcast day. Sitting here alone on this bench all I could think about was how Sotiny might've dealt with this grief and guilt on her own at only sixteen. How so many of her wounds and defences were born out of this ugly loss.

Another raindrop. Had she actually grieved for him or did his ghost weigh on her just as heavily.

"This isn't what you would want for either of us," I said. Tyson had always been happy and care-free, something I'd always wanted to embody myself despite my temper at the time. He had in so many ways shaped who I was today as well.

And I knew he would've been proud of his little sister pursuing her goals and dreams. And it would appear once again, I was standing in the way of that.

I was certain he wouldn't want either of us

suffering. I felt a weight lift off me, as if I'd finally found some resolve that I hadn't realized I was tormented by.

The rain became heavier as I stood up and pressed a hand to his tombstone. I was certain after our fight that day, that we would've eventually made up. We were like brothers and sometimes they fought. I just never got to say that I was sorry. "I'm sorry it took me so long to make amends"

S taying at my parents' home for Thanksgiving and a long weekend wasn't exactly my dream getaway but it was exactly that—a getaway to clear my thoughts. I was grateful to Damon who accepted my need for a few days off and that when I returned, I'd explain everything. Although I suspected he already had his suspicions since it was him who suggested I had the next few days off.

Home. What did that even mean to me anymore? I'd become so caught up in everything with Sotiny that I didn't even recognize myself anymore. I sat in the games room on the second level, staring out at the window across to Sotiny's old home.

My two nieces played a board game behind me with the fireplace crackling in the background. Their chatter came in and out in waves.

My brother, Jack, and father were looking over my dad's new car project in the shed. And my mother and Jack's wife, Susanne, were cooking downstairs. I'd enthusiastically decided to play board games with the kids just to offer a few more hours away from adult conversation. I just needed to check out for a while after visiting Tyson's grave today.

"Uncle Alex," Olivia demanded. "You're not even playing with us." She was only six but had the demanding temperament of any teenager I'd known.

"I'll join in next game, how does that sound?" I smiled.

Susanne crept upstairs, jumping out and scaring the girls. She picked up Lucy who was four and bent over to give Olivia a kiss on the cheek. My brother and Susanne had been happily married for years now. How time had flown. They'd started their own family and I'd started what? A real estate portfolio. I rubbed my face, man, when did I even start thinking about kids?

"Your mother asked if I could swap with you so you can go down and carve the turkey," Susanne said sweetly.

My gloomy-ass attitude wasn't exactly anyone's joy to be around for Thanksgiving but I didn't have the energy to pretend like everything was okay either. But their tiptoeing around me was even more unnerving.

"She wants *me* to carve the turkey?" I clarified. Me, the same man who almost burnt his own kitchen down last week?

"She said you could use the practice?" Susanne said sheepishly.

"Sounds like something Mom would say." I stood up from the cushioned nook and rubbed the girls heads, messing up their hair.

"Hey!" Olivia squealed trying to straighten it again. "You said you'd play the next game."

"I promise once I'm done helping Grandma we'll play," I enthused.

My mother was swaying her hips and humming to herself, as she always did when she cooked. The whole room smelt of different spices and herbs. I grabbed a beer from the fridge and opened it, eyeing her.

"Susanne said you wanted me to practice carving the turkey?"

"Indeed," she said, grabbing a knife for me and pointing me in the direction of said turkey. "Now remember, Alex, there is no right or wrong way to carve a turkey but please let it be somewhat presentable for the photos I'll upload later."

I chuckled. "Still in that cooking group huh, Mom?"

"Well what else do you expect me to do around here?" she whined. I chuckled and gave her a kiss on the cheek. I looked out the window, sighing. Directly across from our kitchen was Sotiny's old room, except now the curtains were closed. So many memories. So many old and new emotions mixing.

The house has gained more damage than it should've in those years. The lawn was overgrown, and parts of the cement cracked.

My mother quietly said, "It's a shame you couldn't bring Sotiny over, dear." She watched me cautiously. "Is she the reason you're in this... mood?" she carefully said.

"No, Mom. Sotiny and I aren't anything, we just caught up in New York when you called that's all."

She gave me that knowing glance and hummed to herself. "It was awful what her mother did to her."

My jaw clenched. Annoyed that my mother didn't entirely drop it but also at the reminders of how awful her mother had been to her all those years. A protective wave washed over me, almost regretful that I could do more for her now than I could have ever back then. Be damned if my parents told me to get involved or not.

"Yea well I don't blame Sots for not wanting to have anything to do with her," I gritted out. I really didn't want to speak about Sotiny right now.

"Even with the cancer thing, that must've been hard on both of them, but I never saw Sotiny visit."

I had the knife suspended over the turkey. "Cancer?"

"Miss Bryer. Sotiny didn't tell you?" By way of my expression, she seemed surprised. "Her mother was dealing with cancer and the town mayor started a charity for her to start the chemo, but it only really assisted the first payment. I dropped by now and then with food to do what I could but she wasn't doing well. She'd mentioned that she'd reached out to Sotiny and she was paying for it all, including the mortgage payments."

My eyebrows furrowed in confusion. She what? She hated her mother so why would she do that? "When was this?"

"I don't know a few years, probably around the time she graduated." She seemed to think on it. "Probably up until about eighteen months ago. The last time I visited and we had tea together her mother was outraged that the payments had stopped coming through. Considering she'd stopped chemo eighteen months before that, I was surprised she still expected it. But you know how Miss Bryer can be, she's a little odd."

I ground my teeth together. "You don't find that strange that she hadn't informed her the chemo had stopped?"

"I try not to butt into other people's affairs, Alex, you know that, especially in a town as small as this."

I stared at their house. When Sotiny's CV had come through our office, I knew exactly who she was from the start. And sure, I might've suggested to Michelle that she seemed like the finest candidate but even then I was confused as to what happened between the five years when we saw one another in Vegas and why she hadn't done anything with her degrees until then. She'd always been determined but now suddenly it dawned on me. If she was paying for her mother's chemo... then she was probably working multiple jobs to cover the costs, just like she'd done to put herself through college.

My blood boiled. For how long was her mother going to haunt her? To ask for more and manipulate Sotiny into believing she was her responsibility. Enough was enough. Fuck Sotiny hurt me, more than I'd like to admit, but if there was one thing I could at least do for her, that Tyson can't do now, it was to set her free from her mother's grasp.

My father and Jack walked in, both giving my mother a kiss on the cheek. My father froze when he saw me with the knife. "Woo there, Chief, why don't I take over here," he joked.

With perfect timing, I gave him the knife and headed for the front door. "Alex, where are you going?" my mother called out.

"To pay Miss Bryer a visit." The words came out like dripping acid.

"Alex, we don't get involved in other people's affairs," my mother shouted out from behind me but I was already gone.

This had nothing to do with meddling. This was about setting a girl free who should've been looked after and held instead of beat down repeatedly. This was about the woman I loved finally being set free from the woman who broke her into a fragment of herself. If I could do only this parting gift, no matter how much it hurt, I would. Because I was stupid enough to do anything for her.

Chapter 40

Sotiny

Alex disappeared for the rest of the week and by Thursday I was certain he never wanted anything to do with me again. While everyone else might've visited family and celebrated Thanksgiving, I holed myself up in my apartment and attempted seven times to pick up my book and continue reading it with no success. I just couldn't focus. Everything felt like a chore, waking up, keeping to myself at work as best as I could with minimal discussion, but still maintaining the polite smiles and replies right on cue.

I stared at my messy apartment and the pile of comic books that had fallen over. Well, I certainly wasn't going to any weekend event in Boston now that was for sure.

I'd drafted the same email over and over again to send to Crystal Publishing. Every time I wanted to hit send, I wavered on my start date. Although I'd spoken to Michelle about some options and Crystal Publishing was flexible as to whether I started before Christmas or in the New Year, I found myself inclined that the sooner I was out of the office the better.

I couldn't stand the idea of being around Alex or anywhere in the same building as him. I didn't want to ever face him again, not with that pitiful expression and pure disdain he held for me. And in a way, it felt like exactly what I deserved.

I knelt beside the comic books, shuffling them into a pile. Decidedly, I peered under my bed at the few boxes I'd kept when I first moved in. Looking around the crammed and messy apartment I suddenly felt like an outsider. This had never been my home. I was up until one month ago content by the idea of moving to another city. Doing anything that I had to, to get where I wanted to be. To selfishly put myself first. And although my logical brain couldn't comprehend these feelings that were getting in the way, I knew I was only prolonging the inevitable, just as I had with Alex.

I dragged one of the boxes out and put the first

comic book in and then the second. Slowly, I began packing them away. There was something almost therapeutic in the act. I scanned my entire apartment. I could pack most of this now and leave all of this behind me. I could start anew.

Chicago it was. And the sooner the better. That left only two things. I pulled out the small manila folder hidden away in my stack of books. When I opened it, it revealed Alex's and my wedding certificate with the little vending machine ring tucked in the corner. One, I'd have to file our divorce with his signature. Two, I'd have to endure one more event with him as our project came to a conclusion, and I'd leave right after. I took a deep breath. Both of which would break me. But I could get through this. I *would* get through this.

Two weeks later, I'd finalized everything. Christmas decorations flooded Manhattan in the peak of the festive season. I'd organized a flatmate online in Chicago until I found myself a new place in the New Year. And purposefully booked my flight to leave the night of the event welcoming

Hayden Zilch officially into the *Be True* family and the sports magazine kick-starting in the new year. And lastly, everything that I'd subscribed to that kept my life in any routine was cancelled.

The life that I'd built here in New York was as easily disassembled as if I'd never been here at all. The only thing that remained yet to be undone was that husband of mine. With divorce papers close to my chest, I dared a knock on Alex Fields's door. This was the last thing I'd ever ask of him. This would be our ending.

On the last Monday I'd ever work at *Be True* magazine, I strode into Alex's office and shut the door behind me. He looked up at me and then back to his work. Those bulky shoulders sagged over his desk as if he was trying to hide away further from me.

"I heard through the grapevine that you're leaving tomorrow night after the campaign?" he said through gritted teeth. He leaned back in his chair clasping his hands together. I hated how he played power moves. Even now. But I supposed I was no different.

"I didn't want to waste any time with the opportunity Crystal Publishing offered me." Sure, they offered me until the New Year but there was no need for me to be here anymore.

"I'd heard Michelle invited you to their Christmas dinner, as well. I suppose though since you're not going there's no reason for me to cancel."

I offered a sharp smile. I bit back every hurtful expression and word that sprung to the surface.

"Up and gone so fast. Three weeks, huh? Must've been desperate to get out of town."

With an ache in my chest, I pointed my nose higher. It felt wrong and bitter fighting him like this. Every part of me fought the urge to throw myself at him every day. And yet, I couldn't allow myself to take that slippery next step. Because if I did, I'd never leave. I'd never say goodbye. I'd never put my dream first. Quietly, I said, "Well there's nothing keeping me here."

I could see the flicker of pain pass over him before that foreboding expression frosted back over. This wasn't the Alex I knew, nor the one anyone else saw. What I'd give to see that cocky dimpled smile one more time. But I was the reason we were here, and I was paying the price for that. Our walls were once again our redeeming features. "Except this."

I placed the divorce papers on his desk. He eyed them before that burning glare trailed back up to me, those green eyes penetrating. Stubble crept through on his usually clean-shaven face.

Ah this was the ugly side of Alex Fields. Hurt him once, shame on me. Hurt him twice... But hurt him thrice... All this hatred was all mine to have. *I'm sorry, in the end I couldn't offer all of me,* I thought inwardly.

"Leave it with me and I'll hand it over tomorrow night at the campaign," he said, adjusting himself in the chair.

"Why can't you just sign it now?"

"Because I like to read over the contracts I'm signing, Sotiny. Especially this one."

My jaw dropped. "What you think I'm trying to screw you over or something?"

"I never said that. It's been six years since you've clung to those divorce papers, hasn't it? The very first day you arrived here and realized I worked here as well; you served me with the exact same papers the next day. What's one more day longer? Is it that painful being married to be?"

"Don't do that," I whispered.

"Don't do what? State the obvious?"

"Fine as long as it's done by tomorrow. *Please, Alex.* "I won't be coming back to New York. I think it's time we leave the past in the past. And step forward. For both our sakes."

"Well, you've always been good at that haven't you?" he gritted.

I bundled my hands together, consciously not biting my thumbnail. I wanted to scream at him. Throw every fucking thing here in this room. But I knew it was partly true. And I could admit to at least that. "Yes," I agreed, then turned and walked out.

Chapter 41

Alex

I straightened out my black shirt and suit for the fourth time in what felt like ten minutes. I'd downed a whiskey in the back room before guests began to arrive. The grand hotel and conference room was in a flutter of assembling last-minute details. I sat on a stool, not entirely sure why I'd even come early.

"You look like you're walking into your own funeral," Damon regarded, taking a seat across from me. His gaze caught Clover whenever she walked past, those hawk eyes always attentive and on her. How nice that might've been. Resting on the inside of my pocket was the signed divorce papers I'd promised.

"Don't worry when the camera's out I'll play

happy family, smile and charm all the new clientele. You know you can depend on me for that," I said, looking into my empty glass.

Thoughtfully, Damon offered his whiskey to me. "You look like you need this more than me."

"I'll wait for my next one like a good boy," I tried to joke but it fell flat.

"She really did a number on you, huh?" Damon asked. We hadn't gotten into too much detail, and I certainly didn't tell him about Vegas and our marriage. He did however know about our past. Her brother and all the ugliness in between. Somehow telling him about the marriage didn't seem necessary. Especially considering I fucked it up so badly.

"Yea," I said quietly.

"Did you ever think about going with her?" he asked.

I stared up at him, shocked. "What?"

"Did it ever cross your mind to follow her?" Not that there was any opening there. She didn't even want me in the same room as her, let alone asking if she'd have me back again.

"We've built so much together at *Be True*," I reasoned. "Everything I have is here in New York. And I couldn't do that to you. *Won't* do that to you."

Damon chuckled as he took a mouthful. "I never

said I was letting you quit. But we do have an office in Chicago, Alex. Remember, you helped open and raise it from the ground up. Surely it crossed your mind?"

I'd be lying if I said it hadn't. But everything I had was here.

Damon shrugged. "There are other ways around this. Chicago's what a two, maybe three-hour flight from Manhattan? I don't know all the details between you two but if you're serious about her, Alex, you could always do two weeks there, two weeks here. Hell, you could always transfer. Not that I don't want you here because you're my best friend and despite how much you shit stir me, I'd miss you.

"But I'd be selfish not to point out that I've never seen you in this state over anything let alone about a woman. Are you sure you're willing to give up on it so easily?"

"Easily," I scoffed. Nothing about Sotiny Bryer was easy. That damn wall of hers was near impenetrable. "It's already too late, but thank you, Damon. I appreciate it." I stood up and tapped him on the shoulder. "I'm just going to freshen up. It looks like we might have guests starting to arrive."

I went to the bathroom, hands on either side of the basin, pondering over what Damon had said. Of course it'd crossed my mind. But she'd already made it so clear that what I had to offer wasn't enough for her. Sotiny always wanted to do it on her own, by herself, no matter the better judgement of others. And I just had to learn how to let this thing go. Surely time would fix this. Wouldn't it? But hadn't that been the same thing I'd convinced myself fifteen years ago?

Fuck. I needed to get a grip on myself.

When I finally mustered the effort to walk back out, it was bustling. Within those twenty minutes I'd been gone, the white marbled foyer had filled. Music played amongst the sparkling Christmas décor on display. Familiar faces were already ordering at the bar.

"Oh, Alex, hey!" Cassidy bubbled out, all bouncy blonde curls. The woman beside her was definitely under some kind of incognito. And then I realized exactly who she was, Issobelle Sherain. Famous New York photographer who is also exclusively contracted to *Candice Magazine*—our competition—and of course Clover's friends.

"It's been a while," I charmed, giving Cassidy a hug. "Are you two allowed in here?" I asked skeptically, pointing in Clover's direction. A promiscuous smile curved her lips.

"Yea well like I quit my job at *Candice Magazine* and have decided to go to Canada, so technically I'm not a conflict of interest anymore."

"You're moving to Canada?"

"Oh no just a little holiday until I decide to come back," Cassidy said dismissively, suddenly taking interest in the golden bangles that matched her long sparkly golden dress and waved to order a drink. I looked in Clover's direction who gave me that "she won't tell me anything else either" look. There was something far more sketchy behind the little secret heiress up and leaving than she was leading on. I wondered when Clover would figure out who she actually was and if it mattered to her at all.

"And what's your excuse?" I asked Issobelle. "Couldn't you get in trouble with your contract being at one of our events?"

She shrugged. "I heard there was free booze here, thus the blue wig and shades?"

"Don't you think you should've gone for a subtler disguise?"

"I don't think people are here for me." She shrugged. I always found their friendship intriguing to say the least. The three women were completely different in every way and yet somehow it worked.

I saddled up beside Cassidy. We'd found

ourselves at the same events over the last few months. The last one we'd even challenged who could pick up first. We had to call our prize and go for it. Unfortunately, we were both too preoccupied to ever verify who'd won. "So, who do you have your eye on tonight?" I said looking out into the crowd.

"Eww I'm officially off New York men and have vowed celibacy," she said, folding her hands over her chest defiantly.

Issobelle theatrically choked on her next sip.

"Hey!" Cassidy regarded. "I do have some self-discipline you know?"

"Oh yea, of course. I'm so happy for you," she dryly cheered.

"This is not what my rock bottom looks like. At least I'm not sneaking around in bars with blue wigs on," Cassidy challenged.

"You might as well be with some of those bad dates you'd been avoiding the last few times we went out," Issobelle replied.

Cassidy's face slackened. "I'm soooo going to miss you."

"I know you will."

"I know I will," Clover chimed in. "It's a shame we haven't been able to hang out more."

"Well, I've had a lot on. You've had a lot on with

all you're traveling. Issobelle's been doing whatever it is she does."

She shrugged in agreement.

"So does 'said' celibacy carry over to Canada as well?" I asked curiously. Wow the serial dater Cassidy vowing celibacy, now I'd seen it all.

"There too. I'm just going to focus on me for some time."

"That's good. Healthy, I think." I'd only ever focused and spent time on myself, how that was working out for me at this point, I wasn't so sure.

My gaze gravitated toward the entrance and the long black slick dress that hugged Sotiny's figure. How cruel could she be? She looked like a fucking goddess. *My wife.* And only up until tonight.

She walked in alongside Michelle and Phillip, finding amusement in something Michelle had said. Just like me, she had a part to play tonight, despite our indifferences. We were the head of this project and for *Be True*, we had to look unified.

Always feeling my gaze, those sharp blue eyes found mine. That clever intellect sparkled under dark shades of eyeshadow, only deepening that pene-trating glare of hers. I had to drag my gaze away before anyone noticed the intensity between us.

"Oh, it's so good to see Michelle feeling better,

did you ever find out what the problem was?" Cassidy asked.

"Not yet but she's invited us over for Christmas lunch so here's to hoping we find out some more," Clover commented, grabbing a glass of whiskey for Damon who eye fucked her from across the room.

"Ooh wow isn't Hayden something." Cassidy whistled as he strode in wearing a white suit with Amber and Gregory by his side. "Now he doesn't count as a New York man."

"What happened to your celibacy?" Issobelle dryly asked.

"Shit. Never mind. Don't let me do anything I'll regret tonight," she pleaded.

"So much for discipline," Clover chimed with a smile before walking away and offering Damon his drink and making the rounds with sponsors and staff. A reminder that I should be doing the same.

Chapter 42

Sotiny

I found myself standing to the side with Alex on the stage. In the center and currently under spotlight were Hayden, Michelle and Damon with a round of applause congratulating and thanking them for developing the new sports edition. Alex and I stood as a united front, clapping and smiling together, rewarded for our efforts.

But inside, I was falling apart, barely a tether to keep it all together. I didn't enjoy being in the spotlight, though I wasn't inclined to let anyone else know that. But standing right next to Alex, knowing that he had our signed divorced papers somewhere on him, took away most of my attention. Tonight was the last night. In New York. Working for *Be True* magazine. Standing beside him.

"And if it weren't for either of you two, we wouldn't be where we are today or certainly as quickly." Damon gestured to Alex and me. "Would either of you like to say a few words?"

Alex and I smiled politely at one another and without a second thought he grabbed the microphone. A quick breath passed through me, grateful he'd taken the lead. He was, after all, far more charismatic on stage than I was or ever would be.

"What a huge success and how exciting," Alex cheered. "On behalf of Sotiny and I, a huge thank you to Hayden and his team at Zilch Enterprises." He pointed to Amber and Gregory. "For making this come alive and so quickly as well.

"To Simon our lead columnist and his team for making this possible even with your busy schedule especially going into the Christmas season.

"To all our sponsors and athletes who have made the first few editions something special and believe in our cause, thank you.

"And to Sotiny Bryer." He paused, staring at me. Uncomfortable, I felt everyone's gaze fall on me and refused to break face. "My partner in crime. We might've disagreed on a few things, maybe a lot actually." The crowd chuckled, especially those who worked in the office. "But we make a really good team. And I'm grateful for this time we could share on a very important project before you're new beginning at Crystal Publishing. You will be missed and on behalf of the *Be True* team, thank you."

Everyone cheered, a few whistles even came my way. Damn I needed a drink. I wanted to fade away from all of this attention. Every word he said clipped away one tightened rope at a time, unraveling me.

Lastly, Alex added, "A toast to the Brogardt family for believing in a vision and offering opportunities for not only the company to grow but all of us. Cheers to *Be True* and all that unfolds in its future."

"To new beginnings," Michelle added, holding her glass up. In unison, everyone held up their drink and applauded.

I threw back a mouthful of my champagne, cheering with the crowd in celebration. I felt estranged from it all. It was nice to leave on a high, to have completed something so substantial and new.

"Well done," Clover applauded as I shakily stepped down the few stairs. I recognized one of her friends, Cassidy, who I was certain had worked with Clover at *Candice Magazine*. But the woman who wore a blue wig and shades, well, I couldn't quite put my finger on where I'd seen her.

I put my best poker face on with a polite

expected smile. "Thank you. It's a little bittersweet but glad I could contribute in a big way."

Clover seemed confused. "You always have. I was under the impression when I first came over to *Be True* that you ran half the show," she laughed. She looked down at her wristwatch. I did the same. I didn't have long at all.

I waited until everyone broke out into natural chatter. Nervously, and probably stress-induced, I swiped at one of the caramel tarts that were being served on trays and shoveled it down.

I chewed at my thumbnail, watching Alex like a hawk. He'd said he'd hand over the papers tonight. And I was certain he'd stay true to his word. This was the last thing keeping me here. All of my belongings had been sent off to Chicago. I had nothing left but the clutch I held and the final string attached to this city. And as if knowing, like he always did, his gaze caught mine and he excused himself from his conversation.

I walked down the hall, leading him into a spare conference room that was dimly lit and unoccupied. I couldn't risk the chance of anyone seeing or querying the divorce papers.

I left the door ajar for him, biting at the tip of my thumbnail. I smoothed over my bob, suddenly self-conscious about the dress I wore and how I looked. I didn't even feel this nervous when I went into meetings with Michelle that were with make-or-break clients.

His muscular frame filled the doorway as he slipped into the room. A million thoughts ran through my mind, not about how he'd hand me the papers or what he'd say but all the other things we could do in this dimly little room. My body reacted to his feverishly. I considered how he could bend me over and spank— I cut that thought off and tightened my grip on my dress, hugging myself. I had to restrain myself from doing something stupid like running up to him and kissing him with apologies that I couldn't entirely act on. I couldn't be so cruel as to continue dragging out our feelings. This was a blip, I convinced myself, and I was certain that within a few weeks of living in Chicago, I'd be over it, right?

"At least you didn't drag me into some alleyway, I suppose," he said lowly. I could still see the streak of his green glowering gaze.

"At least," I repeated quietly.

He let out a low whistle, slowly pulling out the papers from his suit jacket. Hesitantly, he put them on the edge of the table between us and stepped back. "I just have one question."

I gulped. No. No more questions. No more temptation or hurtful words.

"Could you ever see a future with me?"

My mouth went dry. At times it was all I could think about. But wasn't it just a fantasy?

At my lack of response, because I hadn't realized I was taking so long to answer, he continued. "Was this month really that bad?" he asked, wounded. "Trialing to have a go at this?" He pointed between us. "At us?"

I could feel the temptation of my bottom lip quivering and the tear that wanted to escape. Why did he need more clarification? Why couldn't he just let me go and make this easier on both of us. But didn't I owe him at least a little of the truth. "No. It's probably the happiest I've ever been." I gave him a bright genuine smile. "And no one will add up to you, Alex Fields. But I want to be selfish. I want to pursue my dream and do what I told Tyson I'd do. And I'm sorry it couldn't work out."

He seemed hurt by the mention of Tyson. The reminder that he'd vowed never to take me to bed. I wondered if Tyson were still here if things might've been different between us. And although I'd asked myself so many questions and variables over the past few weeks it kept, stopping at the same dead end. I had to be selfish.

Quietly, he asked, "Don't you think he wants you to be happy?"

"Who's to say I won't be happy?" My voice was a whisper. A quiet plea for him to stop.

"Because the way I see it right now, baby girl, you look miserable," he said, slowly taking a step and cautiously raising his hand to my jaw. I had the urge to run. To get as far away from Alex Fields as possible. And yet, he'd grown to become my comfort now. I'd become far too accustomed to the sensation and relief when Alex touched me, an intimacy I'd never shared with or known by any other.

I closed my eyes, his touch electrifying and bringing me back to life for the first time in these past three weeks. I wanted to hold onto it just one second more, but found myself saying, "Don't do that," I pleaded. I wasn't immune to Alex Fields's charm. Never had been and never will. No matter how cruelly or how much I pushed him away.

"Why didn't you talk to me about the job? You don't have to do everything on your own, Sots. You don't have to be by yourself. You don't have to be alone. You can have friends. You can build a new family. You can be included in all of these things." All of his words struck like daggers. I despised that he could see through my cracks into every little fear and flaw I've ever known. "You're not some discarded little doll, Sots. You could have us—if you just let it in."

"And would you have come to Chicago with me?" The question seemed to startle him. "Or would you just expect me to be the one to stay? Because that's what is expected of the woman, right? Of the wife?"

He shook his head, disbelieving. "That sounds like your mother's talk."

"Don't speak about my mother!" I pushed him away. "You know nothing about the shit that woman put me through!"

He knew nothing about the times I was terrified of her. Until eventually I just felt numb, making me feel like some broken shell that couldn't connect to emotion like others. Or maybe I was born like that. I didn't know. Tyson and Alex had been my only rays of light and then when both of them were gone, I was left alone with *that* woman.

I'd spent years on myself since, trying to undo her damage. Trying to unhear the words she'd called me and the unworthiness she forced me to feel and believe. Her daily reminder that my brother was dead because of me.

Alex didn't stand down as he gently added, "All this time, I didn't quite understand why you kept running away. Especially when I knew you felt the same for me that I feel for you. What's between us isn't escapable, Sots. It hasn't been for almost two decades. And then it dawned on me when I went back home for Thanksgiving that you're a scared little girl who doesn't want to connect with anyone or only let them in at a certain level that you can monitor. You're scared to ask for help or let anyone know the real you. You're scared to lose control and act on emotions."

Pain. So much fury, fear, and tears crept to the surface and it was insufferable, like it'd choke me whole. All I'd wanted was someone to see me and now I hated every part of its double-edged blade. "Wow, you think because you have sex with me for three weeks that you suddenly know who I am?" I retorted. *Too close. He was too close.*

He let out a sharp whistle. "It's not the sex that I was after from you, Sots, and you know it. And yes, I do think I know almost every little thing there is about you, baby girl. I know that you're allergic to chilli; I know you bite your thumb and comb you're hair when you're stressed or uncomfortable; I know the volume has to be set on an even number whether it's music or TV; you're favourite sweets are vanilla cupcakes with buttercream icing; you're a surprisingly good singer but you only ever sing in the shower but even then you mostly like to dance; you keep your temperament bottled up so people believe you're a sweet-natured girl, just how your mother raised you."

"Stop it!" My heart twisted with a pain so fierce I thought I'd drop dead. This wasn't fair. All I ever wanted was for someone to see me. And why was it precisely the one man I thought I was never worthy of. What I feared the most was he knew me better than I knew myself. And that meant he saw how ugly I was inside. This deep well of hate, regret, and fear that I'd kept buried deep under the surface and for so long, I pushed it down, but by his slightest provocation, it rolled to the surface.

"This was a bad idea. Thank you for this," I said, collecting the signed divorce papers off the table. "I think I should go."

"Wait, Sots!"

"For once, Alex! Please don't follow me!" I begged, that tiny tear finally finding its way down my cheek. Rage fuelled me as I swiped at it. How dare he make me cry! Every seam that held me together felt as if it were bursting apart. Here would be another city I'd vow never to return to with too many painful memories. Because all of it encompassed Alex Fields. "How much more could you try and break me?"

He seemed taken aback by my hatred. Words that weren't necessarily directed at him. But maybe, if anything, they were words I'd always left unsaid toward my mother. It wasn't fair to take them out on him, but these feelings and hatred had nowhere else to go. I had to leave before I said or did anything else because I was completely coming undone.

I stormed out of the room, the clatter of my heels echoing as I walked down the hallway. I found Michelle first, trying my hardest to keep it together. She was laughing at something Phillip and one of the sponsors had said as she turned around and looked at me, her expression dropping.

"Is everything okay?" she asked, concerned.

"It's fine. I just got a message saying there was a crash on the way to the airport and I have to go early," I lied. It was such an obvious lie, but I couldn't be here anymore. "I just wanted to say thank you to you and your family for offering me this opportunity and I'm so grateful to you and your brother. I'll call on Monday from Chicago. Thank you."

Her gaze fell over my shoulder at Alex. As if understanding, without delay she gave me a hug. "Okay and I have some news of my own to catch you up on, so we'll talk then, but don't be a stranger."

I gave her a curt smile and dashed out the door cramming the stupid divorce papers into my clutch.

"Sotiny!" Alex called out from behind. The night air was a cold slap in the face. I looked back and forth amongst the traffic waiting for a time where I could dart through. Maybe a few streets down I could call a cab. A few streets down that weren't near him.

I dashed across the road. "Sotiny!" I could hear him yelling after me.

Before I realized it, I was taking off my heels and running, crashing into people and being sworn at. Tears welled my eyes as I frantically tried to find an alleyway or somewhere, anywhere, to hide. It felt like sharp icy barbs raced up my feet from the cold weather and hard cement, and yet I wasn't running fast or hard enough.

My heart pounded, Alex's voice creeping closer. My breath came in harsh jolts, my body not accustomed to this kind of running. Faster. Harder. I just had to hide and push all of these feelings back down where they belonged.

"Sotiny! Wait!" The sound of car brakes screeching and a loud thump, froze time. Memories flickered. A red truck crashing into Tyson's side of the car. Darkness. Gone. He was forever gone.

Slowly and horrified, I turned. Alex was hunched over, his hand splayed over the front of the car that had just hit him in the middle of road.

"Alex!" I screamed, bolting toward him and elbowing onlookers out of my way. "Get out of my way! Alex!" A shrill scream that didn't sound like my own escaped.

He tried to stand, his weight favoring one knee. I gashed my knees on the cold cement, cupping his face. Alive. He was alive. I buckled beneath him, looking up and into his face. "Alex?" Tears welled in my eyes. Tyson's face and carefree laughter flooded me. I was back in the hospital room, unable to comprehend the news they'd just told me. *Tyson was gone.* He was gone and I was to blame. I couldn't lose anyone else. Tears streamed down my face. All this fear, regret, and pain surfacing with such a force it was exploding out of me in guttural chokes. Alex was all I had. Please don't take him as well. "Alex."

"I'm okay," he gritted out, clutching his ribs. My

hands shook in a frenzy as I clutched onto him for dear life.

"I'm sorry." Tears spilled down my cheeks. "I'm sorry." Everything bubbled over. Every little word and pain I'd held onto all these years. All the things I wanted to say to Tyson coming to the surface, so fierce I couldn't breathe. "I'm sorry." My breathing turned rapid and sharp. "I'm sorry." The repetitive loop became incomprehensible through my shocked stupor and crying.

"Sots?" Alex panicked. I was aware of the spectators standing around us and the traffic that had suddenly stopped. But I couldn't stop. This sheer terror had taken over completely.

"I can't... breathe." Why the fuck was this dress so tight. I clutched onto Alex like he was the only thing keeping me to this world. Dread gripped at me and everything spiraled. My knuckles turned white as I held onto his jacket in an iron grip so no one could pry him away from me. "You can't leave me too." I said out loud, thinking of Tyson. I couldn't lose both of them. Sheer panic and dread tore through me. "I'm sorry for being an idiot," I cried.

"Ssshhhh," Alex said, pushing back my hair. He winced as he tried to stand but I kept him in place.

"Sots, you need to loosen your grip. I'm not going anywhere. Look at me."

He had to nudge my chin. I did as he asked, barely able to make out his face through the horrible blurriness of tears. But there, somewhere amongst the storm, I could see the green of his calm gaze, calling me back.

"Are you fucking crazy running out in front of my car?" the driver yelled.

"I'm sorry." Alex winced, a hand going to his ribs. "Here's my card. Any damages I'll replace."

Slowly, he curled his arms around me and lifted me with him in a sharp painful breath. "Alex. What if you're bleeding inside? What if something's wrong. What if—"

He kissed me then, a sweet tender bruising mark that eased every ripple and tension from my body. My mind went blank. Here. Alex was here with me now. Safe and alive.

He slowly pulled away, his gaze heavily fixed on mine. "I never thought I'd say this to you, Sots, but man sometimes you talk too much."

I hiccupped a shaky breath, confused. He walked us off the street accepting the bottle of water someone offered us and thanked the person who'd called the ambulance. "You don't look okay, Alex."

He was sweaty and pale, wincing every time he moved. "Neither do you. You look like you're having a panic attack." He offered me the water.

My bottom lip wobbled. He grabbed my hand and kissed my knuckles, dragging all my attention to him. People fretted around us, but as always, he somehow made it only about us.

"I think I've broken a rib," he admitted.

"What?" Horror struck me again.

"And also, I bought your mother's house."

"You *what?*"

He tried to chuckle, quickly wincing in regret. "I thought that might bring you back a little."

"Why would you do that? When did you do that?" Suddenly I was sober... and cold in this chaotic street of Manhattan. The traffic continued as if nothing had happened at all. All that remained was a battered Alex and that cocky smile.

"When I returned home for Thanksgiving. You never told me about her chemo or that you paid for it and her mortgage for so long."

"Why did it matter, it wasn't for you to worry about."

"I worry about anything that involves you, Sotiny Bryer. I thought by now surely, you'd see that." He pressed a kiss to my knuckles again. "When I found out I was outraged." He sucked in a sharp breath a jolt of pain running through him. I fretted over him but he raised his hand as if he weren't done speaking. "I hate that woman," he admitted. "I hated how she treated you and how she tried to mold you. And when I found out about you helping her and her taking advantage, I couldn't handle it. Sots, you deserve to be free from that woman. So, I dealt with her."

"You make it sound like you threw her into the bottom of a lake."

His chuckle went abruptly short as he winced. "Tempting," he squeaked out. "I told her I'd buy the home and pay out the mortgage on the condition that she never call you again, nor could she text or even so much as breathe your name," he hissed with a fiery passion.

I sat there clutching at his hands, surprised and scared of the fierceness he openly threatened her with. His hand cupped my jaw again.

"Why would you do that for me?" My bottom lip wobbled. So many times I'd thought about what it'd be like without her. And often the fear of having no one at all crept in. No matter how much I despised her, she was all I had. Followed closely by guilt, especially during her chemo that I had to look after her in Tyson's place.

"Because, Sotiny, I'm ridiculously in love with you, and I have been since I was sixteen. And if this will set you free, I'll do it a thousand times over. But selfishly, it would appear this time, I'm not quite ready to let you go myself."

Tears spilled over my cheeks as the sound of sirens came toward us. "Why are you making this so hard for me," I squeaked. "I want you more than I'd like to admit. But I've always wanted this job too, Alex."

"I know," he said, stroking my cheek and pushing back my hair again. "So why don't I come with you to Chicago? Even if it's only two weeks at a time?"

"What?" My voice was barely audible.

"I don't care about New York, baby girl, it's not home to me if you're not there. I realized this the moment you gave me an inch and I was willing to run a mile with it."

The ambulance pulled up on the curb in front of us with people pointing in our direction as witnesses began telling them what had happened. We must've looked strange, right after his accident with me having some sort of panic attack, and yet for the first time in a long time, we seemed to be having a civil conversation.

"Don't go tonight. Wait until after Christmas and start in the New Year so we can go together," he said, slowly rising and holding his ribcage and wincing. I tucked under his shoulder, not that I was any support considering our height difference.

Everything felt like a blur as the ambulance officers escorted us into their vehicle. I thought about my flight and clung to him like he was my salvation. "Are you serious?" I asked weakly. My legs were wobbly, and I realized I was cold. "Because you know I'm moody and I have outbursts and—"

He leant down and kissed me again, this time with a possessive fierceness. He winced as he pulled back, those green eyes boring into my mine. "Sotiny Bryer, I knew and agreed to all of those things the night I said 'I do.'" He held out his hand, offering for me to join him in the back of the ambulance. "What about you? Are you willing to give this a second chance?"

I stared at his extended hand, so used to holding myself back. So accustomed to finding the reasons as to why I shouldn't. Right now, I was a mess, and there was a chaotic heaviness that loomed over me from all these exposed and raw feelings. But I knew, wholeheartedly, that I would be safe with Alex and I didn't want to face this trauma alone. Above all, I loved him. I curled my fingers around his, stepping into the ambulance van. "Yes."

As he took a seat he looked down at my filthy feet. "Where are your shoes?"

"Um." I looked out the back of the vehicle before they slammed the doors shut. "I don't know exactly."

He chuckled, immediately wincing as another dart of pain shot through him.

"Stop trying to laugh so much," I hissed at him. I fretted, unsure as to what I could do to help.

The whole time the paramedics spoke to him he held my hand, rubbing his thumb over my fingers contemplatively. My heart hammered as slowly, he pulled me under his shoulder and tucked me in tightly, as if he too were scared, I'd try to run away again.

Despite his immediate pain, he wasn't letting me go. And I felt warm and safe in his embrace. Everything was a whirl, but for the first time, I finally had hope that anything was possible between Alex and me. I'd become too tired from running and he'd finally caught me.

Epilogue – Alex

"And where do you want me to put this stuff?" I asked, carefully dropping the box into the middle of the hallway. Sotiny had already fluttered off into the office. I was certain this was a box of comics considering its straightforward title "comics" on the side. Shuffling around things with two broken ribs was a lot more strenuous than I'd like to admit.

"In the office?" she asked.

"Or how about I order a full-length shelf across here?"

She darted out of the office in our Chicago home with a beaming smile. She stared at the bare wall I pointed at in the living room near the fireplace. "With the ladder looking thing attached to it?" she asked, big-eyed.

I chuckled. "If that's what you want."

She sweetly tucked herself under my arm. "I'd like that very much." She pressed a kiss under my jaw, still tiptoed.

"And how did your new boss go with the news about our honeymoon?" I asked.

She dragged the heavy box of comic books to the corner of the room. It was like watching someone struggle to pull their own body weight across the wooden polished floors.

"She was okay with it, surprised that I was married since I hadn't mentioned it. But then again no one knows."

I grinned. "Except for when we let it slip at the Brogardts Christmas lunch, huh?"

"Well except that. I mean I think it was a bigger surprise to hear that Michelle and Phillip are expecting a baby."

My eyebrows shot up. Yea that was definitely a relief and a surprise for everyone sitting at that table. I just wondered how she'd cope without having a glass of her favorite red during the festive season.

Sotiny called out, breaking my mischievous thoughts. "Maybe we should do a small wedding when we get back from our honeymoon in France, for your family's sake?" she asked, propping both hands on hips and out of breath.

"Shouldn't we do the wedding before the honeymoon then?" I said raising one eyebrow.

"No way," she gasped under the boxes weight. "I'm not delaying Paris calling out my name any longer. Also is Damon still okay with you doing two weeks here in Chicago and two weeks in Manhattan with the news of Michelle's pregnancy? He might need you more than ever."

"He's fine with it and if I need to stay for a few more weeks I might. Although two weeks away still sounds like too long. So he might be okay with it but I'm not," I grumbled, pulling her into me, ignoring the sharp pain that followed through.

"Maybe space is good for us," she joked.

"I've already had more than enough space from you." I grabbed her jaw, holding her into position as I kissed her. Mine. Ridiculously fierce and maddening. And all mine.

She pushed me back with a mischievous grin. "We shouldn't, we have a meeting soon to pick out our rings," she said with a heated gaze.

"I also know you didn't put that butt plug on the kitchen counter for display," I murmured.

"I was trying to be subtle and conscious of your weakened feeble form."

"Feeble?" I choked out on a laugh. "Let's see how feeble I am." I bolstered her up and over my shoulder, a squeal escaping her as I slapped her ass hard. I collected the butt plug from the kitchen table before dragging her into the bedroom.

It was different to New York and although I'd miss the hustle of Manhattan, I had everything I needed here. I had her. And we had us.

—

To connect find Kia on www.kiacarrington-russell.com

Thank you so much for reading my book. If you enjoyed this book, I'd love to hear your honest thoughts in way of a review. It not only helps support my writing but also gives me important feedback on how you felt and connected with the world and characters. I love connecting with my readers and would appreciate if you could take two minutes to leave a review or rating. Thank you so much and I hope you are having a wonderful day!

About the Author

Raised in the Darling Downs Region in Queensland, Australia, Kia Carrington-Russell, began writing as an angsty teenager, finding a passion for exploring creative realities and world building at fifteen. After graduating high school she decided to pursue a career in freelance journalism, and quickly amended that dream with something that made her heart beat faster and her mind race—fiction. With fresh eyes she went over her first manuscript, "Possession of my Soul" and began her publishing journey in 2014.

With a recognizable style of kick ass heroines, fast-paced action, and romance that dances from light to dark, she's been pronounced "the new up and coming author to look out for" and her writing style as "hauntingly beautiful."

Carrington-Russell's books have been recognized on multiple best-seller lists, most noticeably, her "Token Huntress" and "My Escort" series for which she's won numerous awards and notable reviews, including "Reader's Favorite" 5 star reviews for

"Token Huntress" and "The Shadow Minds Journal."

She has a firm belief in giving back to the writing community—sharing knowledge, promotions, and opportunities that might help other authors reach their readers, including running her own YouTube channel, Bound by Books, where she interviews fellow authors and other industry professionals.

With years in various industries, climbing the corporate ladders, Kia has now settled into a full-time writing career as a successful author and is always looking for the next adventure. She's travelled the world for both business and pleasure, including living in Edinburgh, Scotland for the past year.

Now back in her home country of Australia, she takes her Cavoodle, Sia along morning walks on beautiful coastline beaches, building worlds in the sea breezes and contemplating where she'll go next.